## The Little Derringer That Could . . .

The man at the coach's far end shouted something unintelligible above the din of the train's wheels and hammering connectors, and came running along the aisle.

Longarm slipped his double-barreled derringer from his vest pocket. He had to keep the shooting to a minimum or an innocent bystander was sure to take a bullet; he had to dispatch each of these men as quickly, efficiently, and brutally as he could.

He extended the derringer straight out in his right hand, thumbing both hammers back, his own heart thudding insistently as he steadied a bead on the man's chest. He couldn't let the man trigger the scattergun and send several hundred steel pellets screeching through the close, populated confines of the coach car. That meant he needed to make a clean heart shot, stop his ticker with a single .32-caliber slug.

*Pop!*

The slug tore through the man's crisscrossed canvas bandoliers just as he stopped and slammed the butt of his Greener against his right shoulder, narrowing one eye. He jerked back, swinging the shotgun up, and triggered both barrels at the same time . . .

**TABOR EVANS**

# LONGARM

## IN THE LUNATIC MOUNTAINS

**JOVE BOOKS, NEW YORK**

**THE BERKLEY PUBLISHING GROUP**
**Published by the Penguin Group**
**Penguin Group (USA) Inc.**
**375 Hudson Street, New York, New York 10014, USA**

Penguin Group (Canada), 90 Eglinton Avenue East, Suite 700, Toronto, Ontario M4P 2Y3, Canada
(a division of Pearson Penguin Canada Inc.)
Penguin Books Ltd., 80 Strand, London WC2R 0RL, England
Penguin Group Ireland, 25 St. Stephen's Green, Dublin 2, Ireland (a division of Penguin Books Ltd.)
Penguin Group (Australia), 250 Camberwell Road, Camberwell, Victoria 3124, Australia
(a division of Pearson Australia Group Pty. Ltd.)
Penguin Books India Pvt. Ltd., 11 Community Centre, Panchsheel Park, New Delhi—110 017, India
Penguin Group (NZ), 67 Apollo Drive, Rosedale, North Shore 0632, New Zealand
(a division of Pearson New Zealand Ltd.)
Penguin Books (South Africa) (Pty.) Ltd., 24 Sturdee Avenue, Rosebank, Johannesburg 2196,
South Africa

Penguin Books Ltd., Registered Offices: 80 Strand, London WC2R 0RL, England

This is a work of fiction. Names, characters, places, and incidents either are the product of the author's imagination or are used fictitiously, and any resemblance to actual persons, living or dead, business establishments, events, or locales is entirely coincidental.

LONGARM IN THE LUNATIC MOUNTAINS

A Jove Book / published by arrangement with the author

PRINTING HISTORY
Jove edition / January 2011

ISBN: 978-0-515-14881-7

JOVE®
Jove Books are published by The Berkley Publishing Group,
a division of Penguin Group (USA) Inc.,
375 Hudson Street, New York, New York 10014.
JOVE® is a registered trademark of Penguin Group (USA) Inc.
The "J" design is a trademark of Penguin Group (USA) Inc.

PRINTED IN THE UNITED STATES OF AMERICA

10  9  8  7  6  5  4  3  2  1

# Chapter 1

Waking up alone was no damn fun.

That was the first thought, half-baked as it was, to enter the lawman's head as he opened his eyes and sat up in his humble bed in his even humbler digs on the poor side of Cherry Creek.

The room was cold. There was no supple thigh rammed against his own leg to warm him. No well-curved buttock jutting against his crotch, inviting him to some dreamy, half-awake frolic. No cleavage for him to ram his nose down and take a deep whiff of the comforting, milk-and-citrus smell of womanhood that was sure to take the sharp edge off the dawn and the prospect of another long day in the sharp light of the law's demanding service.

Custis Parker Long, known as Longarm to friend and foe, smacked his lips and stared into the dusty light of dawn emanating through his flat's three windows over which he'd forgotten to draw the shades when he'd stumbled in late last night. Early this morning, rather. He'd

stopped off at the Black Cat Saloon for a few drinks to cut
the coal soot.

*Shit.*

He'd figured on taking the day off. Maybe even two or
three days off. His last job had gone two weeks over what
he'd expected, and when he'd ridden the Burlington flier
into Union Station at ten thirty last night, he'd felt as
though he'd been tied to a plank with a rabid bobcat. That's
what finally running down the paper-hanging ring over
Nevada way had been like, especially after the counter-
feiters had gotten wind the federals were onto them—he
was working with two inexperienced deputy U.S. mar-
shals out of Salt Lake—and the owlhoots had lit off from
Las Vegas toward Mesquite by way of the Valley of Fire.

That had been a lot of fun, trying to haze three killers
out of those hot rocks and hidden canyons under a sun
that would have fried an egg atop his head through his hat
in under a minute.

"Could have been worse," he could hear his boss,
Chief Marshal Billy Vail, say. "Could have had to chase
'em across Death Valley." And then, of course, Billy would
lean back in his high-backed, overstuffed leather chair and
start gassing about his own experience, twenty or thirty
years ago, of single-handedly running down the worst killers
to draw a breath on the western frontier through Death
Valley at high summer with a single canteen only half-
filled with tepid alkali water.

Shit.

Yeah, he'd figured on a couple days off . . . until last
night a ticket agent in Union Station had slipped him a
characteristically cryptic, pencil-scrawled note from Billy
Vail: *My office. Tomorrow. Eight thirty. (Not a minute later!)*
*Billy.*

Longarm glanced to his left. His visitor's pillow was still covered with sheet, quilt, and bedspread. Not a wrinkle on it.

He'd half hoped that Cynthia Larimer would have been waiting for him here, which she sometimes did when her busy world-travel schedule found her in Denver, holing up at her aunt and uncle's sprawling, opulent digs on Sherman Avenue. Cynthia's uncle was none other than General William H. Larimer himself, considered by most to be Denver's founding father. Cynthia, being the apple of the Larimers' eyes—their own daughters were plain, plump, and dumber than whiskey corks—spent considerable time at the Larimer estate, riding the general's Thoroughbreds and Tennessee trotters and hauling her easel off to nearby creeks and prairies to paint plein airs in oil, which she often showed in galleries and even sold, though she didn't need the money.

All of this when she wasn't stealing away to haul her "friend" and "bodyguard" Longarm off to the ballet or opera or some long-winded, mind-numbingly boring symphony he wouldn't have been caught dead at had he not known that the most delectable piece of female flesh in the western hemisphere and above the tropic of Capricorn was sure to reward him with a long, sexual, no-holds-barred wrestling match that would have withered a weaker a man's heart and was sure to wrap her lips around his cock and suck with such force as to cause his eyes to pop out of their sockets.

But the second blow of his late homecoming, after the note from Billy, was that she hadn't been here.

No letters from her had awaited him, either.

That's when, crestfallen as a brokenhearted birthday boy, he slinked off to the Black Cat for shots of Maryland rye.

He hadn't seen Cynthia in a long time—several months, in fact—and he was beginning to wonder if on one of her international forays she hadn't gotten herself hitched to a prince or a count or some such. Likely, she was attending art shows and string quartets in Amsterdam or Paris with a bearded, manacled, moneyed foreigner in full royal regalia, and onlookers were dropping dead at just a glimpse of the full-breasted, stygian-haired temptress. Armies were detonating cannons in her honor, and fleets of warships were hanging flags over their gunwales in the hopes she'd blow their captains a kiss.

*Fuck.*

Longarm groaned, threw the covers back from his lean, broad frame that, hard and corded and bulging with muscles and the puckering knots of healed bullet and knife wounds, was a testament to his hard-fought years as a federal lawdog. He smacked his lips again, opened and closed his eyes, swept a lock of brown hair back from his forehead, and dropped his bare feet to the floor.

The boards were cold. Cold bed, cold floor. And here it was only August. What a long, cold winter he had in store for him. Of course, there were other women, but once a man has partaken of the best beyond imagining, there just wasn't much left to hope for.

Marriage to the girl had never crossed his mind. Well, maybe it had *crossed*, but as briefly as a shooting star across the firmament. He and Cynthia both knew that a union between a lowly, salaried public official and a Larimer heiress would have been akin to wedding a prized, pure-blooded poodle to a mutt that fed from gut wagons.

Besides, marriage likely would have taken all the intrigue and thus the lusty venom from their proscribed trysts in the unlikeliest of places including horseback, Aunt May's rose garden, and once—and for almost the final time!—under the general's own desk in his library/office.

Longarm's heart skipped a beat when he remembered the girl's lips and tongue working his rock-hard staff while the general and Chief Marshal Billy Vail had walked in on them during a Christmas party at the Larimer estate. Longarm had conversed with both men while lounging back in the general's chair, his trousers bunched around his boots. Cynthia, unseen beneath the desk and between his naked knees, had continued working him devilishly, thoroughly enjoying the danger as well as his own trepidation while he'd carefully maintained a nonchalant expression in spite of her sucking and chewing him almost raw, as though he were one big, human lollipop.

He chuckled now as he splashed water in his porcelain basin and started a whore's bath. That had damn near been the end of them. No telling what the general might have done had he come around behind his desk and found Cynthia with Longarm's cock between her sensuous lips. Might have had a stroke. Or, as pie-eyed as he was from the Christmas punch, he might have grabbed one of his foreign-made hunting rifles or shotguns down from his wall cabinet and filled Longarm so full of holes he wouldn't have held a teaspoon of his prized Maryland rye.

It had been a horrific, exciting time. He'd relive it on his deathbed, like as not.

Well, all over now. Sure as shit in a stock corral, he thought a half hour later, pulling the door of his flat closed behind him and canting his snuff-brown, flat-brimmed hat at a rakish angle—Cynthia had gone and let someone with as much money as her own family make her respectable.

Leaving Longarm not only unrespectable, but alone and wretched.

Loneliness nipped like rabid lobos at Longarm's heels as he made his way down the outside stairs of his land-lady's three-story house and started through the cool of a late August morn for downtown Denver and another assignment—one that, if there was a merciful God in heaven, would be his last.

"How's it hangin', Henry?" Longarm asked fifteen minutes later as he pushed through the door into Chief Marshal Billy Vail's office to see Billy's prissy assistant hammer-ing away as usual at his newfangled typing machine.

The clattering stopped as long, pale fingers lifted from the keys. The bespectacled young man, who appeared as though the sun had never once caressed his tender skin, leaned back in his chair and craned his neck to look at the clock on the wall above the door of Billy Vail's inner sanctum.

"Let's see . . . you're three minutes late. But that's early for you, isn't it, Deputy Long?"

"This ain't the mornin' to start givin' my shit back to me, Henry." Longarm kicked the door closed behind him, dropped his saddlebags onto a chair, leaned his Winches-ter '73 against the wall, and sailed his hat onto the hat rack to his right. "I'm as wrung out as a cat in a cyclone. What's that you're typin' there? That for me?"

"Yes. I'm almost through."

"Where's he sendin' me this time? Let's see, it's get-ting kinda late in the year. Dakota Territory? Billy always likes sendin' me way up north when the snow's about to—"

The door to Billy Vail's office opened with the chief's titles stenciled in gold leaf on the frosted glass panel, and Billy poked his pudgy-faced, balding head out. "Long-arm, get your ass in here pronto!"

Billy pulled his head back in but left the door standing half open behind him. His bespectacled secretary gave a humorous snort as he resumed hammering away on the infernally loud typing machine, the clattering of which always caused Longarm to grind his molars. Longarm shoved Billy's door wide and stepped into the office nearly filled with a leather-upholstered desk the size of a wagon bed and which was buried under reams of paper and cloth-covered ledger books, as well as carbons, envelopes, federal Wanted circulars, old letters, hidden or disarranged tintypes of Billy's wife and kids, pencils, and pens—all covered by cigar ash so evenly sprinkled that it appeared to be lying there on purpose, as though spewed by some nearby miniature volcano.

Near Billy's green-shaded Tiffany lamp, pen holder, and inkwell was a wooden ashtray filled to overflowing with more ashes as well as mashed cigar stubs resembling shriveled banana worms. A lit cigar perched there now, sending up a thick web of smoke that started curling about halfway between the desk and the lamp's green shade.

"Ah, fuck, Billy," Longarm said. "You must have mistaken me for one of your rookie deputies like Pendleton or Murray. Damnit, I'm one of the old hosses in your friggin' stable, and if you keep workin' me like this, you're gonna have to either shoot me in a few months or send me off to the glue factory!"

Longarm plopped down into the red Moroccan leather guest chair angled in front of the desk, stretched his long legs clad in his customary skintight whipcord trousers out in front of him, and crossed his cavalry boots at the ankles.

"I got in last night at ten thirty!" he added, irked that Billy had distracted himself with the papers he was busily shuffling while completely ignoring his senior-most dep-

uty's reasonable protestations. "I know the wild and wooly
ones are runnin' amok across the West in spite of my own
constant yet futile efforts, but holy shit, I need a few days
off. Hell, how long's it been since I've had a vacation,
Billy?"

"Oh, quit your infernal whining."

Billy tossed a brown cardboard folder across his desk.
Longarm lurched forward to grab it. There was a Wanted
circular secured to the top of the folder with brown office
string.

"You recognize that gentleman?"

"That's no gentleman," Longarm said, scowling down
at the inked visage staring back at him with eyes like
miniature charcoals beneath the slightly curved brim of a
high-crowned, Montana-creased hat. "That's Henry 'the
Hammer' Beecher out of Canada. Ah, shit. He's out?"

Longarm had delivered Henry "the Hammer"—so
named because he'd used a ball-peen hammer to murder a
parson's wife teaching him Sunday school when he was
only twelve—to the Canadian Mounties seven months ago.
The Hammer had been wanted in Canada though he'd
been arrested here in Colorado Territory on the less severe
charge of selling whiskey to Indians, and an extradition
treaty had been negotiated.

"Escaped last Tuesday."

"I knew that pen up to Moose Jaw wouldn't hold him."

"Well, you were right." Billy sighed.

"Don't tell me. They think he's in Dakota, Montana
Territory, maybe even Minnesota. Somewhere so far up in
the fuckin' northland that about two weeks from now I'll
be wakin' up with my pecker froze to my thigh. I'll have
to boil water to thaw it out." Longarm slapped the folder
against his knee. "Damn those Canucks!"

"Well, you would have to boil water to thaw it out . . . if that's where I was sendin' you."

Billy leaned back in his chair. He had an inscrutable expression on his pasty, pudgy face and in his watery blue eyes slightly magnified by his round-rimmed, gold-framed spectacles that, like everything else in his office, were lightly filmed with cigar ash. He leaned forward to pluck his cigar from his ashtray and began to puff, drawing the smoke far deeper into his lungs than his long-suffering doctor would have approved of.

Longarm frowned, cocked his head to one side—skeptical, cautious. "You're not sendin' me up there, to run the Hammer down again?"

"Nope."

"Where are you sendin' me?"

"Lunatic Mountains."

"The Hammer's in the Loonies? I thought he mostly stayed up north of the Missouri River on account of him havin' so much family up there."

"He does. And as far as we and the Mounties know, the Hammer is indeed in Dakota. Probably getting ready to settle in with one of his Dakota harlots for the winter."

Longarm raked his befuddled gaze across Billy's desk, to a window, to the banjo clock on the wall, and back to Billy again, his confused frown cutting deeper into his leather forehead. "Now, wait a minute. You're confusing me. If the Hammer is up Dakota way, and my assignment is runnin' the son of a bitch to ground, why are you sendin' me into the Lunatic Mountains right here in *Colorado*?"

"Because that's where your precious Miss Cynthia Larimer is headed."

# Chapter 2

The name sent a mini lightning bolt through Longarm.

Now Billy really was confusing him. No, the man was toying with him, taunting him, adding injury to the insult of his being called in here on the heels of his dragging his sorry ass back to Denver late last night. Frustration rippled like stomach acid up the lawman's chest.

"Because that's where Cynthia Larimer is headed," Billy had said. Or Longarm had thought that's what he'd said.

The federal badge toter opened his mouth but before he could speak, Billy removed the stogie from his tobacco-speckled lips and glanced at the file on Longarm's lap.

"That there is the assignment I was intendin' on givin' you until you were requested in writing by the General William H. Larimer himself to accompany his favorite niece on vacation to see her uncle and cousins in their lodge way up high in the Lunatic Mountains of south-central Colorado."

Billy rested his head back in his chair, stuck the stogie

back in the right corner of his mouth, and puffed with satisfaction. Longarm stared at him. He must have been in shock because the room was suddenly hot, as though a fire had been over-stoked, and it was tilting and turning every which way.

He must have heard wrong. Lack of sleep. Yeah, that's what it was. He was sleep-deprived. And too much rye on top of it.

"Get it through your thick head, Deputy," Billy said, removing the stogie again and glowering through the smoke haze above his desk in frustration. "You've been assigned to act as bodyguard to the general's niece on a two-week, all-expense-paid vacation. Surely you remember the general's niece. The globe-trotting Miss Cynthia? The one you've been using for a human pincushion, fucking seven ways from sundown at every opportunity behind the general's and dear, sweet Mrs. Larimer's backs . . . until I was sure, just as sure as the sun would set and the moon would rise, that you were gonna be shotgunned months ago!"

Billy had worked himself into a red-faced tirade, jutting his dimpled chin and double neck over his desk and poking his stogie at Longarm in exasperation. "Instead, you lucky bastard, you're being invited by special written request to further fuck that delectable forest nymph to your heart's desire on *paid fucking vacation*!"

Longarm swallowed. He was beginning to believe what he was hearing, but he was still skeptical. "No shit?"

Billy's laughter dwindled until he settled back in his chair, spent. "No shit." He sighed. "Go with God, Custis."

"I'm on vacation?"

"Yep. And it ain't even an official vacation. Officially, you're on assignment to guard the niece of General Larimer."

"Holy shit in the nun's privy."

"That was my sentiment exactly when I opened the request letter." Billy puffed his stogie and shook his head. "The luck of the wicked, I reckon. But all joking aside, Custis—I hope you enjoy it. You've worked your ass off of late, and I haven't been able to give you the vacations you've so richly deserved. Well, here's a plum for you finally. Just do me a favor and don't kill yourself toilin' between that debutante's spread knees. I need you back here in two weeks. I'm sending Pendleton after the Hammer, but I'll need you out in the Injun Nations by the first of next month."

Longarm was still staring at Billy in shock. He hadn't fully comprehended.

"Cynthia? Vacation?"

"You got it. You and her together in the Lunatics." Billy jerked with a start, craning his neck to look at his banjo clock. "Holy shit, old son—you better haul ass. Her train's due to pull out at nine thirty, and she's down there waitin' for you in her *own private car!*"

Longarm leaped out of his chair. "Well, hell, Billy— you could have given me a head's up!"

"Wanted it to be a surprise. Now, go, go! Get *outta* here!"

Longarm flew out of the main office and grabbed his saddlebags, rifle, and hat. Henry had just stamped a document in the open folder on his desk and now with a sniff the secretary held the folder up with one hand while shoving his spectacles up his pudgy, pale nose with the other.

"Your official assignment orders and travel vouchers, Deputy Long."

"Expense-paid vacation," Longarm snorted, still trying to get his mind used to the idea he was about to see Cynthia, whom he'd thought he'd never see again. He was not only about to see her again, but he was running away with the girl, just the two of them alone, on a mission of pure carnal bliss. "I'll be diggity-dog goddamned!"

He stuffed the folder in his saddlebags, set his rifle on his shoulder, and left the Federal Building at a heel-grinding sprint. Union Station was a good mile from the Federal Building, but Longarm managed to leap on the back of a firewood wagon headed in the same direction, straight down Sixteenth Street.

The firewood seller took him as far as Writer's Square. From there he hitched a ride for another block on a coal car before his friend Munson Bridges, a cattle buyer from Cheyenne who was heading back to Union Station to hop the northern flier, welcomed the anxious, breathless lawman aboard his rented hack.

While Bridges made small talk and bragged about the killing he'd made last night playing blackjack with his wood-selling brethren, Longarm consulted his old, dented railroad turnip.

Nine twenty-six.

Shit.

When the hack had to stop for a big Dougherty freight dray pulling away from the vast loading docks abutting the Grubmann & Finn Mercantile Company on Market Street three blocks from Union Station, Longarm cursed again and leaped down to the cobblestone street.

"Much obliged for the lift, Munson," he called, throwing his saddlebags over his left shoulder. "I reckon I get that fast on foot from here!"

Setting his repeater on his other shoulder, he lunged forward in another tooth-jarring sprint. He could hear a couple of locomotives whistling and chugging, hear the pops and sputtering of the heavy steam release valves, see the great billowing puffs of coal smoke rising behind the massive sandstone façade of Denver's crown jewel of modern architecture—Union Station. The black hands showing against the white face of the clock atop the vast central watchtower showed 9:30.

Longarm dug the low heels of his cavalry stovepipes deeper into the cobbles as he crossed Wyncoop Street and dodged travelers coming and going through the station's four sets of massive oak and glass-paneled doors. He already had his ticket, so he ignored the tellers' cages and sprinted through the great smoky cavern that was the station itself, which smelled of sweat and varnished wood and tobacco smoke, and flew through the station's rear doors and onto the rear platform.

Amidst the dragonlike breathing of the locomotives, there was the ubiquitous warbling of pigeons flitting about and walking along the cinder-paved platforms, pecking peanuts and bread crumbs and outrunning unsupervised children dressed in travel duds. There were only two trains on the tracks directly fronting the station's rear doors, but neither appeared to be outfitted with Cynthia's own private railcar which, if Longarm remembered correctly, sort of resembled a caboose with extra fittings of glass and wine red curtains over the windows.

"Custis!" a girl screamed.

Longarm looked around. Roughly a dozen travelers milled about the two trains sitting before the station.

"Custis!" the girl screamed again, more desperate this time.

More desperate now himself—Longarm would recognize that voice if he never heard it again for a thousand years—he jerked his head this way and that, sliding his eyes around, trying to pick the stygian-haired Larimer queen out of the crowd. Just then he heard the squawking and hammering of iron wheels and the loudening chugs of a locomotive under fresh steam, and he looked left until he could see beyond the end of the first train in front of him.

A third train was pulling out of the station. Cynthia stood on the rear vestibule of her private car, hitched in front of the red caboose, which her own car dwarfed. She was waving her arm anxiously, her straight, Indian-black hair blowing in the wind.

Longarm threw up his own arm in an acknowledging wave and took off running once more.

*"Cust-issss, hur-reeeeeee!"* Cynthia cried.

"I am hurryin'," Longarm muttered as he ran along the cobblestone platform, his rifle bouncing on one shoulder, his saddlebags bouncing on the other.

As he ran, he could see Cynthia's train rolling down the tracks, the engine chugging and throwing great billowing clouds of coal smoke into the air from the big, black, diamond-shaped stack. The slack in the car couplings was taken up with hard slamming sounds, and the wheels shrieked like demons.

Longarm jogged around the end of the train immediately in front of him, which was longer than the second one, and leaped the second set of tracks. Rather than run down the ties that would have made for even more difficult maneuvering, he ran between the two rock-mounded railbeds, his free arm pumping. His lungs burned and his ankles were twisting in his boots that, with their low heels, were relatively easy on the feet though not made for this kind of wear and tear. As he drew within thirty yards of Cynthia's train, which he gained on gradually, his watch slipped loose of his brown wool vest pocket and flopped against his cartridge belt.

Longarm ignored it. The double-barrel derringer in the opposite pocket would keep it from flying free. He kept his eyes on the hourglass figure of Cynthia Larimer, who continued to beckon to him and reach for him over the brass side rail of her canopied rear vestibule. Her ravishing body was fairly bursting from a cream taffeta basque with modestly puffy sleeves and a skintight beehive waist that accented her flat belly, and with a low-cut bodice that proudly revealed a good half of her ample, perfectly proportioned bosom.

Longarm's mouth watered as he stared at those incredible tits heaving with encouragement as the brass handrail shoved them up high under Cynthia's long, creamy neck.

Her hair blew out farther around her head with each small but not insignificant burst of the train's speed as it angled out away from the station toward the tawny buttes southwest of the Denver stockyards. With each thunderlike chug, Longarm increased his own speed, heels pounding the rocky gap between railbeds and avoiding the occasional bits of trash, including bottles and airtight tins.

"Faster!" Cynthia fairly shrieked, reaching out farther over the rail.

Longarm gave a final burst of his own steam though he momentarily lost not only Cynthia but the entire train as a sudden downdraft of wind dropped a heavy, fetid cloud of coal smoke over him. The smoke, dark as sudden night, filled his lungs. It was hot and pungent and he could feel glowing cinders singeing his face, even saw one settle on his right shoulder and begin to lift a small tendril of smoke from the seam.

When the cloud folded back away from him, he threw

his arm out and saw that his hand was only a foot from Cynthia's outstretched own. He handed her his rifle and kept running. She turned and leaned the rifle against the wooden front wall of her coach, then extended her hand to him once more.

Longarm was chugging now. Bells of exhaustion tolled in his head so that he couldn't even hear the train above them.

Cynthia couldn't hold his weight for more than a second, so when he thrust his hand forward and she grabbed it, he used it to balance himself for the half second he needed to toss his saddlebags over the rail beside her and onto the vestibule floor. At the same time, she gave his other hand a pull. She was stronger than she looked. She pulled him up close enough to the train that as she stepped back, he got both hands on the vestibule rail.

He ran several more steps, trying hard to keep his footing on the rocky bed with ties jutting toward his boot toes, and flung his boots up and forward while hoisting himself with both arms. Relief swept through him as the toes of both boots found a purchase on the iron-grilled walk, and he pulled himself up until he was looking down at the girl staring up at him from the opposite side of the rail, her hair whipping out behind her in the wind.

"Custis!" She squeezed her hands together beneath her chin, then flung both arms around his neck, pulling his head down and closing her mouth over his.

God, what lips the girl had.

Like ripe cherries soaked in the finest liquor melded from the peat of Scottish bogs and aged in cedar casks.

He held her tight, amazed as always to feel how slender she was, how warm and supple in his arms, her heaving bosom pressed nearly flat against his chest. Longarm wasn't too exhausted from his run to feel the old, elemental pull in his groin. He couldn't wait to get this girl into her coach, tear the fancy dress off her body with his teeth, and haul her delectable, porcelain-pale nakedness under the covers . . .

Just as her warm, wet tongue began to slip between his own lips, Longarm heard a loud, harsh voice-clearing.

Cynthia jerked with a start and pulled her mouth back away from his. A pink flush rose in her perfectly chiseled, creamy velvet cheeks, and she clapped a hand to the small gold broach attached to her white silk choker, casting her wary gaze behind her.

Still on the far side of the vestibule rail, the heels of his boots dangling over the platform's edge, Longarm glowered at the hefty female figure standing just outside the open coach door.

It was hard to tell the woman's age. She was stocky as the wife of a German dairy farmer, with a double chin, and sort of cow-eyed. She wore a black dress in several layers complete with a brown cape and a brown scarf pulled loosely over her dark brown hair that sat close to her scalp with a couple of unattractive curls hanging low along her chubby white jaws and near the corners of her fat-lipped mouth as though to point out their lack of feminine appeal despite how thick and pink they were.

The large, brown eyes bored frankly into Longarm from suety sockets.

Longarm scowled at Cynthia. "Who's this?"

"Uh, this," Cynthia said, glancing demurely between Longarm and the hefty old broad in the doorway. "This, Marshal Long, is Beatrice Wannamaker. My . . . my . . ."

Cynthia didn't seem to know how to finish, so the stout war hatchet nearly filling the doorway, settling a thick shoulder against the frame and crossing her arms disdainfully, did it for her: "I'm Miss Larimer's chaperone, Deputy Long. How wonderful to meet you."

# Chapter 3

Longarm's heart stopped beating for about two minutes.

He felt it start up again with a slow, dull thud against his rib cage when Mrs. Wannamaker invited him inside the coach and out of "this galldang Colorado wind," and he dropped warily into one of the plush chairs that adorned and lent more than a modicum of comfort to the otherwise most comfortable and well-appointed railcar that the lawman had ever seen.

He'd never seen the inside of Cynthia's car, and he couldn't help thinking, as he looked around and the delectable Miss Larimer poured them each a drink, that, with all the pillows and two sturdy chairs and the roomy sleeping quarters with a canopied bed at the far end, it would be a grand place for a tussle with his favorite debutante.

Had Cynthia not been traveling with a chaperone, that was.

Longarm shook his head as if to clear it of chaos.

"I didn't know that you traveled with a . . . uh . . ." He suddenly found it hard to pronounce the word.

"Chaperone," Mrs. Wannamaker finished for him, sitting on the orange brocade fainting couch to his left, which was abutted on her far left by a miniature potted palm.

"Yeah, that," he said, accepting the cut-glass goblet of Maryland rye that Cynthia proffered. "I didn't know . . . you traveled with one." He smiled to try to cover his exasperation and disappointment and lifted the glass to his mustached lips.

"Oh, Mrs. Larimer insisted, of course!" intoned Mrs. Wannamaker, whose belly bulged out from the waist of her dark dress, the size of a fully primed fire hose. "She would never allow a niece of hers to travel unattended. God forbid. Not with a man, surely!"

Mrs. Wannamaker's laugh, like the rest of her, was unattractive. She had a strangely smooth, soft voice. Almost like the voice of a girl. Her eyes were large and doughy but not at all in an attractive way. They looked like eyes that could pinch down into acrimonious slits at the drop of a hat. Longarm wasn't sure of the woman's age. Her skin was smooth, like that of a lot of fat people. And of a creamy texture. She wasn't out in the sun much. She could be anywhere between thirty and fifty, and she'd likely stay this way, with maybe only a touch of gray here and there in her hair, until she was ninety.

The woman's mocking laughter died with soft little snorts, which she tried to muffle with a pudgy fist.

"Did you want anything to drink, Beatrice?" Cynthia asked, indicating the silver tray adorned with liquor bottles that sat on a low, cherry table beneath the car's right-side window.

"Oh, not for me. Especially not spirits. Not that I'm prim, you understand," the chaperone hurried to add, holding up a waylaying hand at Longarm. "No, not at all. Except for wine on occasion, the tanglefoot has just never agreed with me, that's all. You go ahead, Deputy Long. Go ahead and enjoy. You may take the bottle with you, if you like, when you retire to your own quarters."

Longarm glanced at Cynthia, who returned it. Of course, a chaperone would never let a male—even one guarding the body of her chaperonee—anywhere within range of a blown kiss after sundown. But the woman's statement served to highlight the crux of Longarm's disappointment. He could see that Cynthia was equally disappointed though she pasted a good-humored little smile on her full-lipped mouth, her cobalt blue eyes flashing radiantly as always. The line of her jaws seemed a little tense, however. As though she were hoping that Longarm would take the unexpected news of the chaperone's presence as good-naturedly as possible.

*And not throw the bitch over the vestibule,* the lawman thought.

He was miffed. Damn miffed. And he had good reason to be. Of course, Billy Vail had known how this all laid out. That was obvious now. Imagining how Longarm's mission was going at this very moment, the sunlight-starved, stogie-puffing chief marshal was probably beating his feet on the floor beneath his desk in uncontrolled laughter. While Henry tittered into his hand in the outer office.

"That's all right," Longarm growled, throwing back his entire glass of rye in one swallow. "I have my own bottle in my saddlebags."

He handed his empty glass to Cynthia, then rose, tossing his saddlebags over his shoulder and picking up his rifle from against the wall. "I reckon I'll head on over to my quarters . . ."

"Yes, that would be one of the coach cars," Mrs. Wannamaker said with a fake hospitable smile glowing like pennies in her dark eyes. "So sorry the train doesn't have a Pullman, where you could kick back and get comfortable, Marshal Long. But then, bodyguards really shouldn't get too comfortable, anyway." The corners of her revolting mouth quirked upward. "Should they?"

She's onto us, Longarm thought. Somehow, she knows that if she weren't here, Cynthia and I would be doing it doggie style right where the old hag was sitting now. The dried-up hag was having one hell of a good time spoiling their fun. Probably because she never got any such fun herself . . . and never would.

"I should say they wouldn't." Longarm glanced at Cynthia. "Where we switching to the narrow-gauge train?"

"Walsenberg," the girl said. "They'll be switching the wheels on my car to accommodate those of the mountain line."

"Well, then, Miss Larimer," Longarm said, all business. "I'll be seein' you in Walsenberg. Meanwhile, I'll try to find a seat in the next car up. I judge it won't be very full this time of the week. Either of you need anything, just fire a pistol out the window and I'll come a-runnin'."

He gave Cynthia an ironic wink. She turned her mouth corners down. He pinched his hat brim at Mrs. Wannamaker, the lady gave him a curt nod, and he went back out the door he'd come in. The private car had only one door and was connected via two catwalks along its outside walls to the vestibule of the coach car ahead of it.

Longarm made his way along the narrow walk, grumbling and holding his hat on his head with his free hand, swaying to the train's movement and blinking his eyes against the coal smoke gushing back from the Baldwin locomotive about six cars away. He pushed through the door of the coach car and stopped suddenly, blinking his eyes as though to clear them, and found himself staring down the yawning maw of a .45-caliber Colt Army revolver.

"Where the hell'd you come from, slick?" the man behind the gun asked. "From that car back there?"

He was in his late twenties, Longarm judged. He wore a high-crowned black hat and a cream duster. He was so near that the lawman could see each individual freckle on the man's pale face, and every hair in his long, red sideburns that were trimmed sharp as scythe blades at their ends, angling toward his lips.

Longarm hesitated, holding the man's blue-eyed gaze.

"We'll check it out in a minute, Clyde!" said another obvious train robber who stood at the opposite end of the car, holding a double-barreled shotgun up high across his chest.

Meanwhile, a big, broad-shouldered man with long, greasy black hair was moving down the center aisle toward Longarm, ordering all the passengers—the car was only about a third full—to throw their money and valuables into the gunnysack he was holding open.

"Only a supply car back there," Longarm said. "I just come up from havin' a smoke with the brakeman in the caboose."

"Supply car?" Clyde grabbed Longarm's Winchester, stepped back, and canted his head this way and that, peering through the glass panel in the vestibule door. "I reckon I'll be checkin' it out." His cobalt blues strayed to Longarm and narrowed. "No offense, but you don't look like the trustworthy type and that car looks a mite fancy."

Longarm was glad he hadn't worn his badge, which he

hardly ever did unless he was making an arrest. Sometimes anonymity was the lawman's best strategic weapon. If they took his wallet, however, they'd seen his U.S. marshal badge tucked inside it. And they wouldn't like it one bit. Probably shoot him without another thought.

And Cynthia was back in her private car—rich, beautiful, and defenseless against three gun-hung desperadoes.

He'd really stepped into it now . . .

"Give me that six-shooter," Clyde barked as the big, black-haired gent continued to make his way down the aisle, occasionally stopping to argue with a passenger reluctant to give up his or her valuables. He paused to pat down a man in a green-checked suit and matching bowler, to make sure the salesman wasn't withholding.

"All right, all right, take it easy." Slowly, Longarm snaked his right hand across his belly and lifted his walnut-gripped .44-40 from its cross-draw holster on his left hip. He held the gun out toward Clyde, shifting his own gaze between the big man moving down the aisle and the man at the car's far end, who was obviously watching for trouble coming from one of the other cars.

Were there more robbers on the train? Longarm wondered, his anxious mind switching back into lawdog mode after the troublesome findings in Cynthia's private coach. Or were these three working alone? If so, he had to take them down fast, before they moved on to Cynthia's coach. When they saw the special cargo the car was carrying, they'd likely go far beyond robbing the moneyed niece of the even wealthier General Larimer.

"What else you got on you?" Clyde said, snapping the fingers of the free hand he held out in front of Longarm. "Come on, come on. A well-dressed gent like yourself has gotta have somethin' beside lint in them pockets."

Longarm shifted his eyes back to Clyde. "Sorry," he said, trying to buy some time. "I ain't been paid in a while. The train ticket done took my last two dollars."

"Don't bullshit an old bullshitter, amigo. You start dippin' into them pockets, every last one, or—"

"Hey!" the big, long-haired man shouted in a low, guttural voice. "You holdin' out on me, bitch!"

Clyde glanced over his shoulder. Longarm began to make his move, but then Clyde, sensing it, glanced at him and stepped back and sideways, keeping his cocked Colt aimed at Longarm's belly. Clyde turned back to where the big man had stopped about halfway down the aisle and was staring down at a pretty young woman with curly, dark brown hair and wearing a loose linsey tunic and a pleated gray skirt. She sat beside a blond man close to her own age, who was clad in a floppy-brimmed hat, grubby coveralls, and a ratty suit coat. Farmers, most likely.

The woman had a silver chain around her neck. Whatever was attached to the chain was inside her tunic, and she was clutching her hand over the tunic as she gazed defiantly up at the big man who held a pistol on her and her husband, who was red-faced with terror.

"Hand it over, bitch! Hand it over now!" the big man ordered, shaking his open hand in the woman's face.

"No! I can't! My mother gave it to me just before she died!"

"Please, Alma!" the farmer cried in a faint Scandinavian accent. "For God's sakes, give it to the man before he shoots us both!"

"No!" she screamed.

She clipped the scream, however, when the big man jerked her suddenly up by her arm. He'd pulled her up and out into the aisle before she seemed to even know what had happened to her. He jammed the gun at her face and gritted his teeth.

"Off! Take off the shirt, bitch, or I will shoot you now, blow your brains all over your husband! Is that what you want?"

The woman sobbed and held her crossed arms tight against her chest. A fine-looking young woman, Longarm noted. Curvy and long-limbed. Nice-shaped. A wholesome farm wife probably on her way, with her husband, to visit family somewhere along the Front Range. The lawman's stomach was filling with bile as he realized what was about to happen to her.

He had to make a move.

As though reading Longarm's mind, Clyde looked at him with a hard, knowing stare, continuing to aim the cocked Colt at Longarm's belly. There was something else in Clyde's eyes—the unmistakable gleam of wanton lust.

Oh, Christ. They weren't all going to take her, were they? Right here in front of her husband?

Longarm became keenly aware of the double-barreled popper in his right vest pocket, connected by the gold-washed chain to his watch. If he could only get his hands on the derringer . . .

"Please don't hurt her!" the farmer cried, sitting up now with one knee on his seat and staring with beseeching at the big, black-haired hard case.

"I woulda just taken the necklace," the big man said, grinning down at the farmer's pretty young wife. "But now I want her to take off her shirt and show me what's down there!"

He grinned, showing a full set of big, crooked, tobacco-stained teeth.

"No!" the farmer's wife screamed.

"Please, Alma!" the farmer cried. "He'll *shoot* you!"

Suddenly, the big man rapped Alma across the face. The blow resounded like a pistol shot. Alma jerked back and to one side, eyelids fluttering. The big man caught her by the front of the tunic and gave the garment a savage tug.

There was a loud shriek of tearing fabric.

And then the pretty young farm wife was standing there, dazed, the tunic and camisole at her feet. Her firm, bare breasts stood up from her chest with a small silver cross glowing between them. Her head was down, hair obscuring her face. Her pale shoulders jerked as she sobbed. She lifted her arms to her breasts, but the man gave a whoop and said, "No, no! Don't cover them purty things up!"

He grabbed the small St. Vincent's cross from between her breasts and gave it a hard jerk, breaking the chain.

"No!" Alma cried, bolting forward and thrusting both hands toward the cross. "My mother gave it to me!"

"Alma!" her husband said, reaching for her arm and missing.

The big man held the cross up above his head and laughed at the woman mockingly, staring at her jostling breasts. "Dear ole ma gave it to you, eh?" He laughed harder, then reached down with one hand and grabbed one of the young woman's breasts, squeezing. "How 'bout you an' me go on back to the *supply* car, and I give you somethin' to replace it with!"

Clyde and the gunman at the other end of the car were chuckling, enjoying the show. The other passengers, mostly drummers with a few old folks and a man in a maroon suit who looked like a cardsharp, remained in their own seats. The other women looked horrified, repelled. Most of the other male passengers seemed to be enjoying the show as much as Clyde and the other gunmen were.

Longarm looked at Clyde, who was keeping the lawman in the corner of his careful, nervous right eye. As the big man began dragging Alma toward Longarm's end of the car, Clyde said, "What about the rest of the loot, Chico?"

Clyde must have realized that Longarm might use the distraction to his best advantage, so the gunman sidled a little farther away from the lawman, keeping his cocked Colt aimed at Longarm's belly. Clyde was beginning to look miffed.

Suddenly, there was the click of a latch and the whine of hinges, and Longarm looked to his right in time to see none other than Cynthia Larimer stroll through the coach car's rear door. Instantly, his heart thudded and his ears began ringing, and silently he shouted, *No, Cynthia—get the hell outta here, goddamnit to hell an' back!*

Nothing could have made the situation more complicated for Longarm.

He hoped that Chico and the other train robbers were too distracted by him and the bare-breasted Alma to notice Cynthia's entrance, and that she'd see what was happening and duck quickly back out before they saw her. But then Chico stopped dead in his tracks, and Alma stopped screaming. They were looking at Cynthia, who moved into the car and turned to pull the door closed behind her. When she had it closed, she turned to face the car, giving her head a little toss to throw her black hair back from her face, and started forward.

She hadn't taken one step before, seeing Chico and the bare-breasted Alma, she stopped with a start and a gasp.

Her beautiful lower jaw dropped, and her rich mouth came open, her blue eyes bright with incredulity.

She looked around the car, found Longarm to her left, saw the gun aimed at his belly, and the skin above the bridge of her long, clean nose wrinkled.

"Holy shit," Clyde said in a voice thick with awe. "I do believe an angel just dropped straight down from heaven . . . and right onto my *cock*!"

# Chapter 4

Clyde lowered and turned the barrel of the Colt slightly as his gaze became riveted on Cynthia, who stood statue still in front of the car's closed door.

"Cynthia, down!" Longarm shouted as he smashed his left fist into the side of Clyde's head, splitting open a gash on his ear.

Alma screamed. Longarm chopped his right fist down on Clyde's gun hand, and the Colt exploded into the floor about halfway between the gunman and Cynthia, who, having sized up the situation and was reacting quickly, dropped to her knees. Chico and the gunman at the other end of the coach instantly brought their guns to bear on Longarm.

Alma threw her bare shoulder into Chico. Chico triggered his own revolver through a window on the coach's right side, evoking a bawling wail from an old lady sitting over there and a loud oath from the check-suited cardsharp.

The man at the coach's far end shouted something unintelligible above the din of the train's wheels and hammering connectors, and came running along the aisle. Longarm slipped his double-barreled derringer from his vest pocket. He had to keep the shooting to a minimum or an innocent bystander was sure to take a bullet; he had to dispatch each of these men as quickly, efficiently, and brutally as he could.

He extended the derringer straight out in his right hand, thumbing both hammers back, his own heart thudding insistently as he steadied a bead on the man's chest. He couldn't let the man trigger the scattergun and send several hundred steel pellets screeching through the close, populated confines of the coach car. That meant he needed to make a clean heart shot, stop his ticker with a single .32-caliber slug.

*Pop!*

The slug tore through the man's crisscrossed canvas bandoliers just as he stopped and slammed the butt of his Greener against his right shoulder, narrowing one eye. He jerked back, swinging the shotgun up, and triggered both barrels at the same time.

*Ka-booooommmmmm!*

In the close confines, the blast sounded like ten sticks of dynamite detonated at the same time. There was the following thunder of a good double-pumpkin-sized chunk of the coach's wood-and-tin ceiling being blasted skyward.

Not waiting to inspect the damage to the coach's roof, and seeing in the periphery of his vision Chico disentangle himself from an old woman's thick ankles and knees while she clobbered him thrice with a beaded canvas satchel, Longarm turned to the gunman and took another careful aim.

Chico fired first. His bullet whistled past Longarm's right ear and plunked into the front of the coach behind the lawman. Gritting his teeth, Longarm squeezed the double-bore popper's second barrel. Chico's right eye became tomato juice as it sprayed out the back of the gunman's head. The exiting bullet ricocheted off a suitcase handle and thudded into a narrow beam running along the slightly peaked roof at the car's opposite end.

Meanwhile, Clyde was grunting and groaning as he reached for his dropped pistol. Blood gushed from his badly torn ear, dribbling down along the hard line of his jaw. Longarm stepped on the gun just as Clyde got his hand around the walnut grip. Clyde yelped and looked up, enraged, at Longarm, who sent his other boot smashing into the side of Clyde's head.

Clyde fell back on the grimy floor near an empty seat on the right side of the rocking coach, out cold.

Longarm pocketed his derringer and picked up Clyde's pistol. As he wedged the gun behind his cartridge belt and rolled Clyde over to retrieve his own .44-40, he looked around, relieved to see that none of the passengers looked injured. Alma was sporting a large, red welt on the side of her face where the big man had struck her, and she looked badly shaken as her husband wrapped a shawl around her bare shoulders. But she'd recover. She'd likely be haunted by nightmares for a time, but a hearty-looking girl such as herself would get over the shock of all this.

Cynthia was on her hands and knees in front of the door, looking around with much the same shocked expression as she'd worn before. Walking right smack-dab into a train robbery wasn't something the debutante was accustomed to.

Longarm knelt beside her, placed his right arm around

her shoulders, and gave her a comforting squeeze. "You all right, honey?"

"I think so," she said, straightening her back and looking at him as though seeing him for the first time. "I . . . I was just coming to find you . . . to apologize for Mrs. Wannamaker . . . My God, what just happened here?"

Just then, the coach door opened behind Cynthia. Mrs. Wannamaker poked her head in, looked down at her charge and Longarm on the floor. She arched a disapproving brow. She then raked her gaze around the blood-splattered car with the gaping hole in its ceiling and the three fallen gunman—two dead, a third out like a blown lamp. The woman looked at Longarm again accusingly.

Before she could say anything, Longarm said, "Best take Miss Larimer back to her car, Mrs. Wannamaker. She just sort of stumbled into a bailiwick, you might say."

"A bailiwick, indeed!" said the chaperone, her voice pitched with scolding, her eyes growing wider as she saw the young farmer struggling to keep the wrap over his wife's bare breasts. "Oh, my dear, Cynthia! Are you all right?"

Cynthia let Longarm help her to her feet while Mrs. Wannamaker raked her eyes across the girl as though looking for blood or bruises. Cynthia slid a lock of jet-black hair back from her face, took a deep breath, and put some steel into her voice as she said, "I'm fine. Fine, Beatrice. It's all right. I got in on the tail end of it, I think. It's the poor young woman over there who seems to have caught the brunt of the terrible doings here."

"You ladies go on back to your car," Longarm told Cynthia. "I'm gonna go find the conductor and try to get this mess cleaned up."

"Hold on," Cynthia said, pushing away from him, her

concerned eyes on the farmer's wife, who was now seated, clutching the wrap about her shoulders as she sobbed against her husband's neck.

She started moving down the aisle. Mrs. Wannamaker made a face as she looked once more at the carnage. "Cynthia!"

Longarm plucked a set of handcuffs from his coat pocket, and cuffed the unconscious Clyde's wrists behind his back. As he did, he watched Cynthia stop beside the young farm couple's seat—at least they *looked* like farmers, possibly ranchers—and crouch with her hands on her thighs.

She said something to the couple that Longarm couldn't hear above the thunder of the train wheels and the air whistling through the hole in the ceiling. He could tell she was trying to comfort the poor gal. Cynthia might have been raised in the most splendid conditions imaginable, by one of the most affluent families in the country, but she was far from a callous, spoiled bitch with her nose so far in the air she couldn't see the world, much less have any sympathy for those beneath her social and economic station.

That was one of the reasons, in addition to her carnal cravings and proclivity for all sorts of bedroom high jinx, of course, that Longarm was so attracted to the charming beauty.

As she set her hand on Alma's shoulder and spoke to the poor young woman, Longarm could see that Cynthia genuinely felt the woman's pain and wanted to help.

Longarm felt a stirring of pride for the heiress as he grabbed Clyde by the back of his coat collar and began dragging him past the inert big man with the black hair and a bloody eye socket lying spread-eagle in the aisle and out onto the vestibule. When he'd cuffed Clyde to the handrail—the outlaw was starting to come around, cursing under his breath at the pain in his ruined, bloody ear—the door to the opposite coach opened.

The train's conductor, Sam Cavanaugh, stepped out, rubbing the back of his head. Cavanaugh, whom Longarm knew well from his frequent travels aboard the Burlington flier, was missing his leather-billed hat, and his shaggy, red-brown hair was disheveled. The conductor's round, steel-framed spectacles sagged on his freckled nose. The glasses were also bent out of shape, which had probably happened when he'd been punched in the face. There was a slight notch carved high in the man's right cheek, and the skin around it was discolored and swollen.

"Holy shit, Longarm," the conductor grumbled, blinking his eyes groggily. "I feel like I was hit with a brick. Think it was a shotgun butt to the back of my head. That's one of 'em there . . . obviously. You get the others?"

"Two dead. One's wishin' he was."

"Well, damn, Custis." Cavanaugh chuckled. "Nice to have ya aboard!"

Longarm and Cavanaugh dragged the two dead men out onto the vestibule with Clyde, who soon regained full consciousness and began wailing about the tattoo Longarm had laid on his ear.

Lawman and conductor then managed to get all the valuables the gang had squirreled away in their tow sack back to their rightful owners. When this work was finally nearing completion and Longarm had gone back out to the vestibule to keep an eye on the indignant Clyde, who clutched a handkerchief to his bloody ear as he cursed and howled, the train was pulling into the little town of Colorado Springs nestled in the deep afternoon shadows of the Front Range including the formidable Pikes Peak looming in the west. Snow-capped, the famous peak named after explorer Zebulon Pike, though it could have been named after any of the countless Ute Indians who had scaled its summit to set eagle traps long before Pike ever laid eyes on it, resembled a giant white tooth hovering under a vast periwinkle sky.

When they pulled into the train station at Colorado Springs, Longarm went into the coach to check on Cynthia and her charge, the poor and rather savagely misused Alma. He learned from the woman's husband, who sat looking the worse for wear himself where he'd been sitting before, that "the purty lady in the fancy duds" had coaxed Alma back into Cynthia's own car where Alma could calm her nerves in more comfort than what the far more rustic coach car offered.

"You weren't invited?" Longarm asked.

"Oh, yes, sir, I sure was," the blond young farmer said, smiling benevolently up at the lawman standing over him. Alma's chair was piled with luggage of several shapes and various sizes. "But I don't reckon the older woman—you know, the rather . . . uh . . . large woman—was as eager as Miss Cynthia to have me back there. She looked at me sorta . . . well, sorta wolf-eyed, if you get my drift, Marshal."

"Yeah, I understand. Good way to describe it."

"I'm right comfortable here, though. I was raised on a farm, and the sight of blood don't bother me none. Alma— she's always been a little weak-stomached."

Longarm was about to go back and check on Cynthia and Alma but quickly became distracted again by Clyde's infernal bellowing. And then, as the train's combination

was shuffled about different sidings, and Cynthia's car
was led off to be fitted with narrow gauge wheels, he became consumed with locating the local city marshal and
filling out reports on the train robbers.

Finally, after two hours of tedious paperwork, he con-
cluded dealings with all the local formalities, which in-
cluded making sure that Clyde was safely locked up in
the Colorado Springs jailhouse where he'd await his trial,
and filling out an affidavit, which the federal lawman hoped
would keep him from having to return to Colorado Springs
to testify. He'd put a hold on the mountain train, not wanting Cynthia to get too far out of his sight despite the presence of her "wolf-eyed" chaperone. Nevertheless, he'd
just returned to the station when the narrow-gauge combination, including the Larimer private car, gave a toot and
billowed sooty black smoke as it started west.

The conductor, who was not Cavanaugh but some youn-
ker with a snooty personality and an exaggerated sense of
his own authority, must have gotten tired of waiting. Again,
Longarm had to break into a run, though a shorter one this
time, to catch the damn thing.

Breathless, he made his way down through the coach
cars to Cynthia's private suite, which again was rattling
along between one of three half-empty coach cars and the
caboose.

Cynthia had just stepped out the car's back door, her
black hair blowing in the wind, when Longarm reached it.

"Hello, Custis," she said. "I was beginning to wonder
if you'd bailed on me."

"It'd serve you right. I've never known you to travel
with a chaperone."

"That's because when I've traveled with you, I've always had family along to act as unofficial chaperones."

She smiled winningly. "Mrs. Wannamaker was Aunt May's idea. She's Aunt May's private secretary. Oh, don't be cross with me, Custis!"

Cynthia glanced at the coach's rear windows—one on either side of the door and one in the door's top panel. The gold curtains were drawn. She stepped in close to the tall lawman, snaked her arms around his neck, and pressed her breasts against his chest.

His trouser snake stirred when it felt the warmth of her belly against it.

"Seeing you in action made me quite hot."

"It did, did it?"

"I'm not wearing any underwear."

Longarm tried to respond to that but the words died like dried-up butterflies in his throat.

She rose up on her toes and pressed her succulent lips against his. "I'll make Mrs. Wannamaker up to you," she said, kissing him lightly, gently nibbling his lower lip. "I promise I will. Sooner rather than later."

# Chapter 5

Longarm was ready to bend Cynthia over the vestibule rail of her own private car and take her doggie style, one of their favorite positions. But just when he'd reached around and grabbed her firm, round ass, she gave him a parting peck and pushed away.

"Soon," she said, grinning tantalizingly. "But not now. Under cover of darkness. I have a plan."

Longarm grumbled. His cock was at half-mast inside his pants. She looked down and saw it, and her teasing smile grew broader as she placed her hand over the bulge, giving him a demonic little squeeze and pressing her mouth to his once more.

"Cus-tisss," she cooed. "You're flattering me no end. I'd like you to come in and have a drink with Alma and me. We're having wine."

"On Mrs. Wannamaker's watch?"

"She's only my chaperone," Cynthia said as she opened the coach's door. "Not my lord and master. Come and get out of the wind." Glancing over her shoulder at him, she dropped a cool look at his crotch. "And please don't embarrass the both of us, you animal."

Longarm only grumbled, wishing he had a newspaper with which to cover himself. But as soon as he saw Mrs. Wannamaker sitting in an orange brocade rocker near a window on the car's right side, holding a cup of tea, he felt his pecker shrivel up like an earthworm in a cold puddle.

He relaxed.

Alma was sitting on the fainting couch on the car's left side, her humble homespun dress looking especially humble in the car's exotic furnishings, though Cynthia had obviously given her the crisp white blouse she now wore in place of the linsey tunic that the big man had so easily torn off of her.

Cynthia closed the door behind him, and Longarm removed his hat, coolly greeted Mrs. Wannamaker, who merely nodded and cast him another suspicious look, as though the old bat had been reading his thoughts about bending Cynthia over the vestibule rail.

"Miss Alma," he said, turning to the young woman, who appeared even younger than she had in the harsh light of the coach car, "I just wanted to apologize for what happened back there, and to make sure you were all right."

She'd been looking at him since he'd stepped into the car, but only now did she seem to recognize him. Her brown eyes widened and, setting her wineglass on the table beside the fainting couch, stood up quickly and took long strides until she stood one foot in front of him. "Oh, Marshal Long!"

She threw her arms around his neck and pressed her body tightly against his own. Drawing her head away, she looked up at him, her brown eyes fairly caressing his. "Oh, Marshal, I don't know how to thank you for what you did back there!"

Tears varnished her eyes, and her upper lip quivered.

Awkwardly, feeling self-conscious with the girl continuing to press herself against him, he lifted his arms to give her a neighborly squeeze. "Ah, now, Miss Alma . . ." He frowned. "I don't believe I caught your last name."

"Thompson."

"Now, Miss Thompson, there's no need to thank me. I reckon Cynthia told you who I was. I'm just glad I boarded the coach car when I did."

"I've never been so poorly treated in my life!" she sniffed.

"I'm sure you haven't. And I hope you can forget the whole dastardly thing. Those men were purely depraved, but you can take comfort in knowing that two have been sent to their rewards, which they'll likely find a little hotter than expected. The other one, Clyde, will likely be sent off to ten, fifteen years' hard labor. He'll rue the day he did that to you."

Alma Thompson pulled her body away from Longarm's and crossed her arms on her chest, sliding her indignant gaze between him and Cynthia who stood flanking him. "Tore off my blouse, the one my dear mother made me back on the farm, and exposed me to the eyes of the entire car!"

"They were curs," Cynthia agreed. "But Cust—I mean, Marshal Long," she amended with a quick, nervous glance at Mrs. Wannamaker, "certainly gave them their just desserts!"

"Yes, he did." Alma threw her arms around him once more and sobbed against his chest. "Thank you again, Marshal Long. I just wish there was something I could do to thank you."

Longarm felt a little woozy from all the female attention he'd been getting of late. Not to mention from the press of Alma's firm round mounds against his chest. Hot shame touched his cheeks when he remembered how the ill-treated though well put-together girl had appeared, standing bare-chested before him, perky breasts with dark pink nipples set inside large areolas screened only by the curls of her brown hair.

What a dog he was. He'd best get out of here before his depravity became all too noticeable.

"No need to thank me, Mrs. Thompson. No need at all. Your prompt recovery from the fear and . . . uh . . . embarrassment of the situation will be all the thanks I require."

"Miss Thompson."

Longarm arched a brow. "What's that?"

"Oh, you must think Angus my husband. No, he's my brother. You see, Angus and I are from a farm in Minnesota, near Battle Lake. We're traveling together to look for our pa up around Gothic—you know, in the Lunatic Mountains? I'm not married and neither is Angus. Pa was a little overprotective, you might say, and any suitors Angus and I might have had, living as far out from town as we did, were promptly scared off the place by Pa and his double-barrel bird gun."

She shook her head, flushing and dropping her eyes to the floor. "But that's a long story I won't bore you with, Marshal Long. I'm sure you have more important things to do than listen to me."

"Well, as a matter of fact," Longarm said, glancing at Cynthia and wanting to make a fast escape, "I'd probably best get back to the day coach. I feel a little big and clumsy in here, to tell the truth."

"Oh, stay and have a drink," Cynthia urged, giving his elbow a sharp tug.

He looked at Mrs. Wannamaker, who gave him the evil eye over the rim of her dainty teacup as she sipped from it, sticking out her sausagelike pinky. "No, thanks. I'll leave you women alone."

He almost pecked Cynthia's cheek as he headed for the door—all the more reason to get the hell out of there!—then stepped out onto the vestibule. Cynthia followed him out, closed the door, looked through the window to make sure Mrs. Wannamaker wasn't hard on her heels, then turned to Longarm.

The train was moving slowly up through a winding canyon, mine shacks with their accompanying Long Toms crowding the banks of the stream that threaded the canyon's middle, with here and there a man shoveling dirt from the bank into a wooden bucket.

"I thought I might be able to get away from Beatrice after dark, and we could meet up somewhere private." Cynthia placed her hands on his chest, tugged on his shirt in frustration. "But I can tell the way she's eyeing both of us, I won't be able to get shed of her tonight. But I promise, Custis, we'll have all kinds of privacy once we reach my uncle's lodge. There'll be much to divert her attention . . . as well as ours. We'll have a tryst under cover of darkness—just like old times—long after Beatrice is sleeping with her blinders and earmuffs on."

"I could have done without that image." Longarm kissed the pretty heiress's forehead. "Don't worry. It ain't been much of a vacation so far, but just bein' within shouting distance of you is fine as frog hair with me, Miss Larimer. Besides, the anticipation of meetin' up like 'old times' is gonna make our eventual frolic all the sweeter . . . and hotter."

Cynthia smiled, wound a finger in her hair coquet-

tishly, and rubbed her knee against his. "Will you fuck me
from behind and talk dirty in my ear?"

"Enough of that kinda talk!" Longarm scolded, already
as hot as he needed to be. "I'll see you farther on up the
tracks."

"You most certainly will!" she called as he headed on
up the catwalk that skirted the outside of the car.

Grumbling to himself, half wishing in spite of what he'd
told Cynthia that he'd been given a bona fide assignment by
Billy Vail instead of this so-called vacation, Longarm took
a seat in the coach car just ahead of Cynthia's. The car
had only three other passengers—lean, bony men with ratty
beards and threadbare clothes that were a mix of buckskin
and denim. Mountain men—trappers, hunters who sold
game to the saloons and eateries, or placer miners. All three
were sleeping, heads back with their mouths open, snoring, though the rumble and squeal of the heavy iron wheels
working their way up a steep climb all but muffled the din.

Later, needing a distraction as well as someone to
drink with, Longarm went back to the caboose and found
that the brakemen, like the conductor on the last train, was
also a man he knew. Leech Williams, a good-natured, quick-
witted Negro and former slave from Alabama, was in
similar need of distraction. There wasn't much to do for a
brakeman on these slow, uphill pulls.

Longarm shared a good third of his Maryland rye with
Leech, who returned the favor with a couple of stout cigars he'd been given by a Cuban cigar salesman. Longarm
and Leech spent a couple of hours, until after the sun had
sunk behind the western peaks and the pines turned cool
and dark along the tracks, smoking, sipping the tanglefoot, and shooting the breeze.

When they'd finally climbed to the top of a pass and were starting down the other side, Longarm left Leech to his work and returned to the parlor car to find it all but empty. The three mountain men must have detrained during the combination's only stop, at a little tent camp along the creek.

In fact, the car's only passenger was Alma Thompson, sitting alone about a third of the way up from the car's rear, on the left-hand side of the aisle. She was facing the back of the car, so she saw Longarm as soon as he walked in. There was an awkward moment, the girl flushing and Longarm hesitating, but hell, the car was empty so there was no point in either of them sitting alone.

He used the seats on either side of the aisle to steady himself on the pitching, vibrating floor, and made his way along the car. Shyly, Alma turned to look out the dark window beside her but looked up at him, sweetly bashful, when the big lawman had stopped next to her seat.

"Miss Alma," Longarm said, pinching hat brim to the girl. "Did you lose your brother?"

"Oh, no. He's in the other coach—dead asleep but snoring. In fact, there's quite a few men snoring up there. Those who aren't sleeping . . ." She flushed and drew her denim jacket closed across her chest. "Well, they were staring at me rather rudely, and I've had about enough rudeness for one train trip."

"I figured you'd still be back in Cynthia's car."

"Oh, I didn't want to impose on Miss Cynthia any longer, Marshal. She was very sweet to take me in, and she surely did invite me to stay not only for supper but to make myself comfortable right there on the fainting couch for the evening, but I couldn't impose. I'm afraid that me and Miss Larimer . . . well, we're sorta from different sides of the tracks, if you get my drift."

"Yeah." Longarm smiled. "Me, too."

"Would you like to sit with me?"

"Only if I wouldn't be imposing on you. I take it you'd like to sleep."

"I tried to sleep, but it's no use. I keep seeing that big man's face whenever I close my eyes. Besides, I'm a little distracted by what's become of my father, if you want to know the whole truth, Marshal Long."

Longarm set his rifle and saddlebags in the overhead luggage rack, then doffed his hat and sagged down into the green plush-covered, high-backed seat beside the girl. Longarm himself had been too distracted by his own discomfort in Cynthia's car earlier to have paid much attention to what Alma had told him about her father being missing. Besides, lots of men went missing in the Rockies. Some were found, some were not. Some didn't want to be found.

"Ah, yes," he said now, crossing his legs and hooking his hat on a knee. "You're out here lookin' for your old man. You have any idea what might have happened to him, Miss Alma? Or where he might be?"

The girl shook her head sadly and fiddled with the handle of the carpetbag she held in her lap. "All Angus and I know is his last letter came from Gothic. That's where he went to get into the saloon business with a friend of his he fought with in the Indian Wars. That was Pa's dream after he came out to western Minnesota and found out how cold the winters were—ownin' his own saloon."

"Why Colorado?"

"A friend of his sold a mine claim here—exchanged it, rather, for a plot of ground in Gothic. Pa threw in with him, and they put up a tent saloon. Well, just before he left to go help establish his new business, Pa said he'd send for me and Angus just as soon as he and Mr. Breathitt had made enough money to build something more permanent."

Longarm nodded, thoughtful. It was an old frontier story, one that often ended unhappily.

"Pa wrote me and Angus a letter pretty regular, to let us know how he was getting along. All of a sudden his letters stopped. Weeks went by and then we finally got one from Gothic—only it was from Mr. Breathitt, tellin' us how Pa went out on a supply run to the railhead at Varmint Springs and never came back. His mules came back, and his wagon was found with three full beer barrels in it, but Pa never was."

"No one found . . . ?"

"His body?" The girl looked at Longarm, her brown eyes wide and miserable. She shook her head.

"Anyway, me and Angus sold the farm—most of the money went to back payments on the mortgage—and came out here to look for him. I know what you're thinking. Don't worry, we don't got our hopes up too high. Me and Angus are pretty convinced Pa's dead. But we have to know for sure. And we want to know what happened to him."

"I can understand that."

Longarm looked at her. She was peering out the window, lost in her own thoughts, likely contemplating a cold, dark world through which she and her brother now rode alone, their father having been taken so mysteriously. Since the man's freight hadn't been stolen, the lawman thought, he obviously hadn't been the victim of road agents. The most likely explanation was probably the simplest and cruelest—the man had probably just stopped his team to evacuate his bladder and he'd been attacked and hauled away by a bobcat or maybe even a grizzly.

Why the predator hadn't taken one or both of the mules was anyone's guess—but stranger things had happened. Someone who lived in the area might have happened by, spotted the abandoned wagon with the mules still hitched to the singletree, and, suspecting they'd been there awhile with no owner in sight, simply released them. A humane gesture.

"I tell you what I'll do," he said now, his heart hurting for the girl. "When we get to Gothic I'll introduce you and your brother to the local lawman. I don't know the man but the fact that I tote a federal badge might carry some weight with him. Maybe he'll put in a little extra time on trying to locate your pa. It probably won't be of much help, but I'd like to give you some kind of a hand . . . after all you've been through."

Alma had turned back to him, her delicate lower jaw hanging slack, her eyes wide with surprise. "You'd do that?"

"It isn't much, I'm afraid."

"Oh, but it's so much better than just me and Angus going in there with our pathetic hands out. You're a . . . a right imposing cut of a man, Marshal Long. You'll get his attention, and I bet the Gothic lawdog will try as hard as he can to find out what became of Pa."

"I hope so."

"Oh, thank you, thank you!" Alma threw her arms around him once more. She pressed her body tight against his, and as he tried to not remember how she'd looked with her shirt off, and failed, he really wished she hadn't.

# Chapter 6

A splintery shingle announcing CITY CONSTABLE hung out over the muddy trail that served as Gothic's main street, and pointed up a narrow stairs between a pool hall and a ladies' millinery shop, though Longarm had been in Gothic for a couple of hours now and hadn't seen anything that even came close to resembling a lady—aside from the women he was traveling with, of course.

"Follow me, younguns," the lawman said to Alma and Angus Thompson, who'd followed him out from the train station like lost little lambs in a chill winter rain.

Longarm climbed the creaky stairs and stopped near the top. Before him, in a dim hall that opened onto the creek behind the building, a black-legged red fox was toying with a half-dead rat. The rat was scuttling along the side of the hall as though hoping to escape through the crack beneath the door of the constable's office. The fox had other plans.

It leaped off its hind feet and smashed both its front paws down on the terrified, peeping, scuttling rodent and then, digging its claws into the rat, flipped it into the air with glee. As the rat turned a somersault, the fox's eyes found Longarm, and the hunter froze. The rat hit the crude puncheon floor with a thump and lay on its back, giving little halfhearted peeps of desperation as it jerked its spidery feet, trying to right itself.

"What is it?" Alma asked, leaning to one side to see around Longarm.

"Life in the raw."

Twitching its ears indignantly, the fox decided it had had enough fun and was time to get down to business. It lurched forward, plucked the rat up in its jaws, wheeled, and scampered off down the hall's back stairs, heading for the pines that lined the roaring, white-frothed creek from which the seedy little mining camp had derived its name.

"All clear," Longarm said, continuing up the stairs and knocking on the door as Alma and Angus flanked him, Angus holding his floppy-brimmed, black felt hat in his nervous hands.

Longarm had to knock twice more before a hoarse voice yelled, "Oh, for chrissakes—come on in and get it over with!"

Longarm shoved the door open and poked his head into a dark room that smelled of rancid sweat, chewing tobacco, and liniment. "Get what over?"

"Whatever the hell you're here for!" a voice rasped from the other side of the room, where Longarm, his eyes adjusting to the dusky light, saw a slender, fuzzy-headed figure stretched out on a narrow bed buried beneath several colorful quilts. Only the man's head and craggy, wrinkly face shone above the covers. It turned toward Longarm. The man's expression was not inviting.

Longarm opened the door wider. "You are the constable, aren't you?"

"That's what the sign says, don't it?"

Longarm walked into the room, dragging his wallet and badge out from a back pocket, and held the badge up to where it caught a few washed-out rays of sunlight angling through a grimy window. "Name's Custis Long, deputy U.S. marshal out of Denver. I understand a man disappeared from Gothic a few weeks ago—a saloon owner named James Thompson."

The old man's watery blues shuttled from Longarm to the brother and sister flanking him nervously, then back to the lawman, who stood over the man's cot with his brows beetled with reproof. The fellow before him appeared too over the hill and long in the tooth for keeping the peace in a mining town this far out in the high and rocky. He was probably the most recent badge toter in a long line that had died suddenly of lead poisoning.

Law work out here could often be viewed as a terminal illness.

"Men disappear from Gothic all the damn time," the oldster croaked, throwing his covers back with an annoyed grunt. "Hell, folks disappear in these mountains all the damn time. Some git caught out by Injuns or highwaymen or some fall from high cliffs while lookin' for El Dorado." He dropped his impossibly skinny legs over the side of the cot and pressed one pale, blue-veined, horny old foot atop the other. "I have enough trouble just keepin' up with the ones I see every day without worryin' about them I don't!"

He ran a gnarled paw over the pink crown of his head.

"I can understand that," Longarm said, returning his

badge and wallet to his pocket. "But these two younguns here are lookin' for their pa. He was running a tent saloon with a man named Breathitt. Wilbur Breathitt. You recall either of those names?"

"Thompson and Breathitt," the old constable said, studying Alma and Angus and grotesquely sucking at his empty jaws. "Sure, I remember the names. Thompson disappeared last month from his supply wagon. Breathitt told me all about it. I rode out there and found the wagonload of beer, and no other sign to speak of. I do apologize for your loss, chillens," he told the Thompson brother and sister. "But it's dangerous out here in these mountains. No tellin' what happened to your pa. Animals got him, most like. You don't wanna think on it long cause it shore ain't a friendly way to go, but there you have it."

"They came out here from Minnesota," Longarm said, hooking his thumbs behind his shell belt and staring down at the local lawman with authority. "On the way out here, they endured a train robbery and a savage assault. They're good kids, worried about their father. I told them that when they got out here, I'd make sure their father's disappearance was looked into long and hard, and I'm asking you now, Constable . . ."

"Pike. Jack Pike."

"I'm asking you now, Constable Pike, lawman to lawman, to go back out there and study the situation further. Maybe take someone with fresh eyes. Men don't disappear without leaving *some* sign behind. Now, I know it was a long time ago, and it's likely rained several times since Thompson disappeared, but there's always a chance you could find something that might help in figuring out what happened to him. It's not impossible that he might have fallen down out there, become disoriented from a blow to his head, and is simply lost and living off the land. I'd go out and take a look around myself, but I'm out here escorting a friend of my office to the lodge of Charles Dragoman."

Longarm felt a little sheepish flush rise from his neck. Cynthia was really more of a friend of his own, not of the marshal's office, but General Larimer was most certainly a friend of the marshal's office. Not only that, he was an important man in the territory. And it was the general who had requested that Longarm accompany Cynthia to see her relatives.

The federal lawman also felt a little guilty for not investigating Thompson's disappearance himself, but unfortunately the man was indeed likely dead. And Longarm had no jurisdictional right to investigate anything nonfederal out here. Besides, he really was here to act as a bodyguard to Cynthia Larimer. Kidnapping was a very real danger when it came to one so wealthy.

"Well, it ain't like I ain't already been out there." Pike rose from his bed and grabbed a snoose sack off the cluttered desk that abutted the front wall, under a window. The room obviously served as both office and living quarters. A potbelly stove chugged, a water reservoir steamed, and a black coffeepot sighed, sending up the smell of scorched mud.

Pike offered the snoose pouch to Longarm, who waved it off, then inserted a liberal pinch between his lip and gum, working it slowly as he stared out the window.

"Tell you what," he said, turning to the younguns, "just to stay on the good side of the federals—never know when I'm gonna need their help, don't ya know—I'll send a tracker named Louis Malle out there to have a look around. Malle used to track Utes for the army, and he's in

Gothic now, sellin' mining supplies. But he can still track a june bug across a storm-tossed lake. If your pa's out there—alive or dead, sorry to say—he'll find him."

"Oh, thank you, Mr. Pike!" intoned both Thompson siblings at nearly the same time.

Angus lurched forward, his hat in his hand, and shook the old man's withered paw, pumping it hard. When he'd stepped back, Alma gave the old lawman a hug, and that brightened the old, weathered, sagging face like a Mexican Christmas tree.

"Oooo!" he said, smacking his gums and giving the girl a lusty up-and-down. "That felt right good. Can I have another one o' them?"

When Longarm and Alma and Angus Thompson had left the constable's office, Longarm showed them to what appeared to his trained eyes the safest, most affordable flophouse in the seedy little camp. Then he headed off in search of a bathhouse, as hauling the carcasses of the train robbers out of the coach had left him with the lingering stench of death. The air would have to leach it out of his clothes, but he'd scrub it out of his skin.

As the coach from Dragoman Lodge was not due for another ninety minutes, and Cynthia and Beatrice Wannamaker were safely ensconced in the French Hotel right across from the Gothic Opera House in the camp's bustling heart, Longarm had some time to kill. He found a bathhouse just down the street from the flophouse and paid six bits for a tub in a private room.

The Chinaman who ran the place made good on his promise that the bath would be hot; by the time Longarm had finished scrubbing every inch of his brawny frame with a long-handled brush, he felt like half-melted butter.

He was still standing in the good-sized tub, reaching over his shoulder to give himself a good scrubbing, groaning luxuriously, eyes closed, when he sensed another presence.

He opened his eyes. He blinked. His lower jaw dropped. "Miss Alma?"

It was too late to cover himself. The girl had already gotten a good look at his equipment. He automatically dropped one hand over his privates, anyway.

She stood against the wall beside the curtained door, giving him a funny little smile, arms crossed on her chest. She was wearing a cream cotton dress with a low-cut, lace-edged bodice that pushed her cleavage up invitingly. She'd tied a dark blue bow in her hair, which she'd arranged to hang down around her shoulders.

"I followed you over here," she confessed. "I hope you don't mind. It was the only way I could think of to thank you."

"No need to thank me."

She let her gaze wander across Longarm's broad chest and thick, sloping shoulders before dropping it down his washboard belly to his dong and bulging ball sack. "Oh, I think there is, Marshal Long." She moved forward and stopped within a foot of him, reaching out and letting the back of her hand nudge the end of his cock, which poked out from between his fingers, so lightly that he could barely feel it.

When he did feel it, it felt like a small lightning bolt licking back through his haunches.

"I haven't been with a man in a while. In fact, I don't get many chances, stuck back on the farm as I always am. But when I do get a chance, I don't let it get away. I know that sounds bold, and it is bold, Marshal Long. But it's no bolder than the way you've been looking at me out of the corner of your eye."

Longarm cleared his throat, swallowed. "I'm sorry. I didn't mean to be . . . uh . . . forward."

"Did you enjoy seeing my breasts back in the day coach? When we were being robbed?"

Longarm stared at her.

She turned her palm toward his belly and caressed the end of his cock with her index finger as she rose up on her toes until her lips were only inches from his. "Tell me the truth, Marshal Long, and I'll show them to you again. I don't mind. I know how men are. Pa's had a few hands around the place, and I've gotten to know most of 'em. Even nice girls got needs." Her breath was warm against his lips and nose. Alma spoke slowly, enunciating each word carefully, her eyes soft and teeming with feminine interest. "Go ahead, tell me you enjoy seeing me with my shirt off, and I'll suck your cock like a lollipop, and when your heart's about to burst, I'll climb into the tub with you and let you fuck me raw."

Longarm opened his hand, let the brush drop to the floor. Feeling his heart flutter, he reached up and slid Alma's dress down off of her shoulders and down her arms until her breasts sprang free. She looked down at her chest, as though surprised at how brazen he'd suddenly become, exposing her so suddenly, and arched her brows. She was accustomed to being all innocent and girlish until she was alone with a man; then she liked to have the upper hand while she drove him into a flesh-hungry frenzy.

If she was like other girls he'd known with similar proclivities, she'd also like to have the upper hand during the act itself.

She also probably enjoyed being surprised.

Longarm pinched her nipples. She gasped and closed her eyes. He lowered his head and sucked the left nipple until it was fairly jutting away from the breast, stiff as a sewing thimble. She gasped again, pressed her hands against his head, rubbed his ears. He licked the curved underside of the perfectly shaped orb, lifting gooseflesh from the delicate skin and hearing her groan as she leaned her head back, swooning.

Miss Alma Thompson may have acted like a young girl most of the time, but she was really all woman. A woman with needs . . . Far be it for Longarm to deny her.

The lawman straightened, then lifted his hands once more to her shoulders and gently pushed her down until she was on her knees before him and slathering his cock hungrily, desperately with her tongue. When she had him hot and wet and ready to start pumping seed down her throat, he pulled her to her feet, stripped her bare-assed naked so quickly that she was breathless and searching his eyes as though wondering if she hadn't just wandered into a bear's den.

He pulled her into the tub with him. He, too, was breathing hard. All his frustration over not being able to bed Cynthia at will due to her chaperone's presence had come to a header. "You sure about this?" he said, his voice thick.

Alma had her hands on his shoulders, rubbing him hard. She lowered her hands, raking her fingers across his chest and belly, and wrapped one around the base of his cock, the other around its head. Her hands were warm and slick, sliding around in her own saliva. He could feel her pulse in her palms.

Her voice quivered and her eyes looked almost anguished as she breathed, "Take me, Marshal Long!"

Longarm pulled her down into the water with him, drew her warm rump onto his lap, draped her legs over his shoulders, and took her.

When they were through, there was considerable water on the hardwood floor. She sagged against him, her snatch continuing to contract and expand around him until he slipped out of her. When they'd become disentangled, she leaned forward, wrapped her arms around his neck, and nuzzled him, whimpering.

"Sorry, Miss Alma," Longarm said, standing and reaching for a towel hanging from a nail on a near wall. "I could stay right here and let you repay me for my services all day, but I reckon I got a wagon to catch."

He stepped out of the tub, left her weakly reaching for him. Finally, she drew her knees to her breasts, the nipples of which sloped into the water, and wrapped her arms around her beautiful legs. She rested a cheek on her knees and watched him dress with a dreamy, sated smile.

She sighed and said, "You and Miss Cynthia . . . ?"

"When it's possible."

Longarm saw no reason to mince words. And he felt no shame in his dalliance with Alma. She'd obviously wanted him as much as he'd wanted her, and he certainly hadn't been her first. He and Cynthia were only sometime partners of the mattress sack, whenever she made herself available, and neither had ever pretended any loyalty to the other. Not as far as sex was concerned, anyway.

Cynthia, in fact, would have viewed that even more nonsensical than Longarm. There was no more liberal-minded girl in the northern hemisphere. Or the southern, when she wandered that far . . .

When he'd finished dressing, he went over to the tub, dropped to a knee, wrapped his arm around Alma's shoulders, and planted one last wet kiss on the girl's parted lips.

"Thanks again, Marshal Long," she said as he walked to the door.

Longarm stopped in front of the curtained doorway. "Might as well call me Longarm, since we're sorta friends now an' all."

He pinched his hat brim to the girl and left. She sank back in the tub and loosed a long, sated sigh.

# Chapter 7

Longarm smoked a three-for-a-nickel cheroot while he waited across the street from the French Hotel for the coach from the Dragoman Lodge to arrive.

No point in spending any more time around the obviously disapproving Mrs. Wannamaker than absolutely necessary. He'd be confined in the coach with the woman for the two-hour trip into the high reaches of the Lunatic Range, where the Dragoman Lodge perched atop a high plateau. Besides, the chaperone and Cynthia were likely still in their half-day rented digs, finishing up their own baths in swaddling comfort and sipping tea from fine china, Cynthia no doubt parrying the old bitch's jibes at her choice of bodyguards.

Longarm had no idea what the Dragoman coach would look like, but he knew it when he saw a leather-canopied hack tromp past him from the east, turn at a wide spot in the main street about a hundred yards to Longarm's right, then pull up in front of the hotel. There was nothing else on the street even remotely like it—two overstuffed, quilted leather seats set atop well-braced axles and large, red, iron-shod wheels.

The driver was a big man in a claw-hammer coat over a butter yellow vest and black derby hat, with a corn-flower blue silk scarf wrapped around his neck. Dark-skinned, with long, black, immaculately brushed hair and a hawk-nose, he was obviously an Indian. Likely a Ute from one of the local bands. For a big, lumbering-looking fellow, he climbed with surprising litheness down from the hack's spring seat, then headed on into the hotel be-fore reappearing a few minutes later, Mrs. Wannamaker's two accordion-style suitcases in his hands while a hotel porter flanked the women themselves, carrying Cynthia's own steamer trunk and carpetbag.

Longarm clamped his cigar in one corner of his mouth, adjusted his saddlebags on his left shoulders, hefted his Winchester in his right hand, and tramped through the street's muddy wheel ruts.

"Custis!" Cynthia greeted him with a toothy smile as she stood at the edge of the porch. "Did you have a relax-ing bath?"

The tips of Longarm's ears warmed. "Right relaxin', in fact."

He gave her his hand and helped her down the hotel's broad porch steps. Mrs. Wannamaker was already on the boardwalk, issuing the big Indian crisp instructions for the arrangement of her bags though the man seemed to ignore her as he slid the hefty luggage into the hack's boot any old way he wanted. When he'd finished, the por-ter handed him Cynthia's considerably lighter bags, and he stowed them tight against Mrs. Wannamaker's.

"Just please make sure nothing falls out," ordered the flush-faced chaperone, clutching a tasseled, black cape around her shoulders. "I've a very precious, very expensive cut-glass jewelry case in there, the likes of which I'm sure you've never seen and never will see, being . . . well, being a *native* and all . . ."

"All right, Beatrice," Cynthia said with good-natured patience, hurrying in to rescue the woman from embarrassing herself further. "Let's climb aboard and get comfortable, shall we? If you keep on as you are, this good man is liable to leave us both stranded here in Gothic, and I doubt you'd like that!"

"I certainly wouldn't," Beatrice Wannamaker intoned, casting a disapproving eye at the hotel looming above them. "I've never encountered more squalid furnishings in all my life. A *bedbug* in a place that charges as much as this place does is an affront against all that's *civilized!*"

Longarm and the porter helped the women aboard the hack, Mrs. Wannamaker in the seat up front beside the driver, and Cynthia in the back, behind her chaperone.

When the driver had given the luggage in the rack beneath the rear seat a precautionary rearranging, likely fearing the old hag's prized jewelry box would break and he'd be sent packing back to his buffalo lodge just in time for a cold mountain winter, he straightened and reached for Longarm's saddlebags. He had a gloriously large, flat-featured, broad-nosed, pocked, cherry red face, though he appeared only in his late twenties or so. Like most Indians, his features and chocolate eyes betrayed no emotion whatever.

Longarm rolled the cheroot from one side of his mouth to the other and gave the saddlebag pouch on his chest a pat. "No thanks, amigo. I'll keep these and the long gun with me. Name's Custis Long. You can call me Longarm."

He clamped his rifle under his left arm and extended

his right hand to the Indian, who was every bit as tall as Longarm himself. The Indian shook. Sometimes they did, sometimes they didn't—it all depended on how long they'd been around the white-eyed crowd.

When the man didn't say anything, Longarm said, "You got a handle, friend?"

The Indian had started to turn away. Now he turned back and poked a thick, brown finger behind the blue scarf around his neck, and tugged it down. Longarm couldn't help wincing at the grisly scar—thick, pink, and knotted— that stretched from the bottom of one ear, clear across the Indian's throat and Adam's apple, to his other ear.

Longarm winced, said with chagrin, "Sorry there, friend."

No wonder the man was especially nonresponsive. Someone had hacked out his voice box or vocal chords, maybe both.

Longarm glanced at Cynthia. She stared back at him with a startled look. She, too, had seen the scar.

As the big, silent Indian climbed up into the driver's seat, Longarm tossed his saddlebags onto the rear seat and followed them up with his own bulk. When he'd gotten comfortable beside Cynthia, he set the saddlebags on his lap and leaned the Winchester between his legs, barrel up. He could have stored the gun in the back, but, since this was unfamiliar country, he didn't know what he might run into. And the long gun wouldn't do him any good if he couldn't reach for it fast.

The Indian glanced over his shoulder to see if Longarm and Cynthia were settled. Then he turned forward, released the brake, and shook the reins over the backs of the matched bays in the traces. The hack lurched ahead and the bays were soon trotting.

"Oh!" Mrs. Wannamaker exclaimed with a gasp. "Must we go so *fast?*"

Minutes later, Gothic was behind them and they were winding up into the pine and fir forest of the high, rocky reaches of the mountain range the Ute Indians had long ago named the Lunatics because of the crazed spirits that were said to dwell there.

Longarm took advantage of his close proximity to Cynthia Larimer, with her chaperone sitting ahead of her and facing forward, to lean over, sniff Cynthia's freshly washed hair, and nuzzle her neck. She smelled like fresh cherries and tasted like the sweetest candy.

Cynthia stiffened and leaned away, beetling her brows in a chastising look. Then, her expression turning daring, she glanced at Beatrice Wannamaker, who was riding in the seat ahead with her chin drooping, as though she were nodding off. The big Indian driver appeared oblivious of everything but the winding, rising and falling trail as he leaned forward with his elbows resting on his knees, holding the two-horse team's ribbons lightly in his gloved hands.

Cynthia leaned toward Longarm, threw her arms around his neck, and kissed him with hungry passion. Longarm returned the kiss in kind. He'd gotten his rocks off in the bathhouse with Alma, but he had a perpetual, insatiable desire for this young woman in his arms now. She was like forbidden fruit—a temptress of the most bewitching variety known to man. If he died fucking this girl, he'd die the happiest man since the last well-sated Greek.

Beatrice gave a snort. Cynthia pulled away from Longarm, regarding the woman with a startled look. Beatrice continued letting her head nod and her chin droop toward her opulent, shelving bosom. Longarm reached again for Cynthia, but she swatted his hands away, giving him another brow-beetled look of castigation though it was obvious from the color in her pale, gently tapering cheeks that she wanted him as badly as he wanted her.

Longarm gave a wry snort, then stretched out as much as he could, resting his right arm on the seat back behind Cynthia. He dug a cheroot from the pocket of his frock coat, fired a stove match on his boot heel, and puffed the stogie to life, enjoying the taste of the fresh tobacco along with the smell of pine resin and forest loam that pressed in around him on the chill, late summer mountain air. The aspens mixed in with the conifers on the slopes rising on both sides of the trail were just now beginning to show some color, little pockets of gold leaves here and there.

"So, tell me," he said casually, letting his right thigh rub sensually against Cynthia's left leg, "since I haven't had time to read the file Billy gave me, about this uncle of yours—Dragoman. Who is he and what brought him so far up in the high and rocky?"

"Well, let me see," she said, leaning forward slightly and lacing her hands around her crossed knees concealed by a black wool traveling dress that was just tight enough to give some hint of the willowy suppleness of her long legs and perfectly curved hips. "Uncles Charles is actually only my half-uncle, since he's my mother's half-brother. Mother was raised in England, you know—as was Uncle Charles. Charles came to America about thirty years ago—he must be around sixty now—and that's when I met his children, Cousins Bentley and Lucy. There was another sibling but he was killed in a sailing accident off the coast of Africa. Anyway, Cousin Bentley is sort of a sour apple though he has his own peculiar charm, I guess. He was a sickly child, and his mother spoiled him. Cousin Lucy and I were very close for many years, before Uncle Charles built the lodge up here in the Lunatics and led her away from me."

Cynthia smiled dreamily as she watched the trees and rocks and boulder-lined creeks passing along the trail. She kept her voice up just loudly enough for Longarm to hear above the horses' clomping and the wagon's clattering wheels. "She's quite imaginative, dear Lucy. We got in quite a lot of trouble together, don't you know?"

She gave Longarm a wistful sidelong glance.

"Oh? What kind of trouble, pray tell, Miss Larimer."

"Not *that* kind of trouble, Marshal Long."

"Damn."

"We were young girls, and got into the trouble precocious young girls get into—playing hooky from school to visit the art museums in New York City or to romp about Central Park. A few times we spiked the punch at the Larimers' Christmas ball, but I don't think anyone found out it was us."

"How long has this Cousin Lucy of yours been up in these mountains?"

"Going on seven years. So long that she'd even fallen out of the habit of sending letters for a time. The last one I received from her, the one in which she invited me and any guests I cared to bring to Dragoman Lodge, was her first missive in three years. I was getting worried about her. She was used to the hustle and bustle and culture of a large city before Uncle Charles got into his head he wanted to be a mountain man. It's beautiful out here, to be sure, but living so isolated, year after entire year without even one reprieve as far I know, can do strange things to a person of Lucy's bubbly, precocious temperament. She always wanted to travel to Paris, meet a dashing prince, and attend a music academy."

"Well, maybe she found her academy out here in the mountains." Longarm puffed the cheroot and looked around at the trees and the crystal blue sky over the canyon that they were currently traversing. "As good an audience as any, to my way of thinking."

"Maybe to hers, as well. I just hope her father hasn't made her a prisoner here. I do love Uncle Charles dearly— he's very warm and charitable—but he's always been given to peculiar ideas."

"Such as?"

"Well, before he left England he wanted to be a clergyman. He was good in business, however—English breakfast tea was how he made his fortune, and after that he invested in the western railroad lines. When he came out here, he lived for a time with a Sioux shaman, became sort of an understudy to him, and took an Indian wife. His first wife died giving birth to a fourth child, who died during the delivery."

In the front seat, Mrs. Wannamaker said suddenly, loudly enough for Longarm to hear in the rear seat, "*Uhffftahh-namen!* What is that hideous *smell*?"

Longarm smelled it then, too, and Cynthia made a sour expression, clamping her hand across her mouth. Longarm looked around the trail over which the sickly sweet odor of decaying meat hung like a blanket.

To the left there was a slight clearing in the forest. Back in the clearing he caught a brief glimpse, as the wagon continued along a rocky stretch of the trail, a long, oval-shaped figure hanging from a tree. He couldn't tell what it was exactly, but before the clearing slipped past him and back behind the coach, he thought he could see torn, ragged flesh and blood.

Blood of what?

"You got any idea what that is, pardner?" he asked, leaning forward to speak into the big Indian's ear. He'd forgotten for a moment that even if the man had understood his question, he couldn't respond. At least not vocally. The look the man gave him told him as much—a blank glance of dismissal—before he turned his head back again.

"Probably a hunter's cache," Longarm mused aloud, glancing behind once more. "Game killed and forgotten about, most likely. Looks like a bear or a bobcat had gotten to it."

Cynthia's eyes were watering. "I don't think I've ever smelled anything quite as vile."

"Oh, heavens!" Mrs. Wannamaker exclaimed, holding a lace handkerchief over her mouth and looking behind at Longarm as if for help. "I think it's getting stronger."

"The breeze is behind us," the lawman explained, sinking back in his seat. "It'll pass."

It passed only gradually, but after a few minutes they crossed a saddleback ridge, and the smell dwindled so that Longarm could once more smell the pines and the creek and the delicately pungent tang of turning leaves.

"I've been to many places in the West," Cynthia said as they traversed a broad, open valley with low, pine-covered hills rolling away to each side, with another creek meandering along the base of the western ridge. "But I don't believe I've seen anything quite as beautiful as this."

Straight ahead of them were rocky peaks too numerous to count. Some were already dusted with snow. A couple of clouds, slate-colored in the late afternoon light, caressed their rocky slopes far above the mossy green tree line.

As the trail rose, the valley on the coach's left broadened slightly, and a small lake like a blue crystal nestled at the bottom, abutted on the far side by a steep, conifer-carpeted slope. The rocky shoreline was strewn with the skeletal remains of pines that had likely died when the lake had swollen with spring snowmelt. There were several half-submerged, wagon-sized boulders on the lake's far side.

Its surface was as smooth as polished turquoise, and almost perfectly reflected the sky. The ridge above the lake must have been several thousand feet high, Longarm judged—so high that he got a kink in his neck inspecting it. The trees stopped halfway up, and the rocky slope was pocked, scarred, and troughed from erosion and avalanches. Boulders balanced on outthrust knobs and atop pinnacles and witch's fingers of rock, appearing as though they could be nudged downward and into the lake with the others by the slightest breeze.

To the right, the hills lowered, the forest thinning. Beyond them, the sky had turned the purple of ripe plums, and lightning flashed like sparks from a blacksmith's forge. The breeze had suddenly switched and cooled. Faintly, Longarm heard the deep rumble of distant thunder.

It was a fitting setting for the massive lodge that suddenly appeared before him—grand enough to widen the eyes of the most jaded western traveler and to jerk an amazed whistle from his mustached lips.

# Chapter 8

Longarm had never been to England, and he doubted he'd ever make it. Not on his salary. But he'd seen sketches and paintings and even a few daguerreotypes, and he'd read descriptions in books. He thought now that the lodge looming before him must be an American western version of a grand Scottish castle. A stout-timbered version with a vast wraparound, puncheon-floored porch.

The porch's front timbers were bedecked with elk, moose, and mountain goat horns, animal heads, and ancient Spanish battle implements including battered shields and helmets. There were American Indian war hatchets and arrows, and each corner post of the porch Longarm recognized as Ute Indian welcome totems, the topmost carvings of which warned away ill health and evil spirits.

There were four dormer windows in the building's third story, looking out over a broad, gently pitched shake roof. There were probably six more at the back. In addition to the windows, the roof sprouted stone chimneys, one for every window, which meant there was a fireplace in every room. Each end of the lodge, which appeared a good fifty yards long, was abutted with two more chimneys— massive hearths comprised of stone enough for a couple of modest-sized cabins.

The gargantuan affair was backed by a high, rocky, pine-stippled mountain wall that, from a far distance— if you could see the place from a distance, which you couldn't—probably dwarfed it. But it was the only thing even in this grandiose country given to visual hyperbole that did. The mountain appeared to rise from only a few feet behind the place, but there was probably at least a hundred-yard gap. The outbuildings that supported such an extravagant spread, housing livestock and hired hands, were probably back there, tastefully out of sight and affording front porch spectators an uncluttered view of ragged peaks and pines and the diamond-perfect lake that the coach had just passed.

Longarm, Cynthia, and Mrs. Wannamaker were all gawking with their lower jaws hanging as the Indian driver put the coach up a steep bench and across a stretch of silver-green mountain sage and rabbit brush, then swung it along the gravel drive that formed a loop before the front porch steps.

A man stood on the porch—tall and gray-haired and smoking a briar pipe. He leaned regally against a post, a wistful smile on his haggard, gray-bearded face, one high-topped, lace-up boot crossed behind the other. He wore a ratty buffalo coat open to a wool plaid work shirt and suspenders.

Cynthia waved, and as the Indian halted the coach in front of the steps, the man pushed away from the porch post, smiling, blues flashing warmly. "Well, well, well, if it ain't my little Sinner!"

Cynthia laughed, embarrassed. "Oh, my gosh, Uncle Charles—you remembered. How lovely," she added dryly as the man opened the carriage door and helped her down to the ground where she promptly threw her arms around the man's neck. He leaned back and, laughing heartily, wrapped his own arms around her waist and picked her up off her feet, holding her with great affection.

"And where is Lucy? Will I see her?" Cynthia asked her uncle.

"Of course, my dear, of course," Charles replied.

Longarm grabbed his rifle and saddlebags and met the Indian at the rear of the coach, where the big native began unloading the half dozen pieces of luggage. Setting his saddlebags and rifle down, wanting to give Cynthia ample time to greet her long-lost uncle, Longarm helped, hauling the bags two at a time up to the bottom of the porch steps. By the time he'd stacked them all in a loose pile, Mrs. Wannamaker had been introduced to the man who could only be Charles Dragoman, though Longarm had expected someone a little better attired. Cynthia grabbed Longarm's coat sleeve as he turned to retrieve his gun and rifle.

"And this, Uncle Charles, is my own personal bodyguard—Deputy United States Marshal Custis Long of Denver's First District Court."

Dragoman stepped forward. His eyes were a soft but probing gray-blue. The right socket boasted a long, knotted scar over it—one which traveled down into the man's thin patch-beard, nearly to his jawline. "Deputy Long, welcome to Dragoman Lodge. Happy to have you here."

"The pleasure's mine," Longarm said, giving the man's hand a firm, hearty shake.

He'd vaguely expected an English dandy complete with an opera hat, eye manacle, and pearl-handled walk-

ing stick. But the man before him now was a much more
familiar and welcome sight. Why, Dragoman appeared a
mountain man, every bit as rugged as Longarm himself
had known when he'd come West just after the war. Of
course, the man might only be dressing the part, but the
scar—so savage-looking that it made a muscle in Longarm's own cheek twitch—was all too real. The man had
obviously nearly lost his eye, which was a shade paler
than the other one and tended to roll around, as though
only half-moored in its socket.

"I'm impressed by your choice of bodyguards, Sinner,"
Dragoman told Cynthia. "But how did you lure a U.S.
marshal into your harem? Or is this your uncle the general's doing?"

Cynthia seemed relieved that the man had answered
his own question. "Yes, that's right—the general arranged
for Deputy Long. You know how he is—always doting,
always demanding the best for his daughters and nieces."
She cut several nervous glances at Longarm as she continued with mottled cheeks, "Actually, Longarm has been
in my employ for quite some time. Whenever I'm in Denver, I manage to borrow him from Chief Marshal Vail's
office long enough to escort me about Denver's social
functions. Kidnapping is always a threat."

She cast her bodyguard, who stood stiffly grinning beside her, another sidelong look.

"Denver has social functions?" Dragoman asked, incredulous, as the Indian wheeled the coach around the
side of the house and out of sight behind it. "Why, the last
time I was there, the brunt of its socializing went on over
at a place called Wilomena's Do Drop Inn, on the west
side of Cherry Creek. Had some high-busted Negro girls
over there, and the half-breeds weren't half bad, neither!"

Mrs. Wannamaker broke in, her chortling voice pitched with disgust. "If you wouldn't mind, sir, but I'm feeling a little faint from the ride. Your driver insisted on driving *awfully* fast, and I could use a few minutes to settle myself."

"My apologies for Wolf's driving, but I assure you, you were in very good hands. I also apologize if my language gets a little off-color. You see, I don't entertain much way out here—simply wouldn't care to even if I had more opportunities—and I'm afraid I might be a bit foreign to the current social graces."

Dragoman drew an arm around Mrs. Wannamaker's shoulders, another around Cynthia's, and began leading both women up the broad, split log steps.

"That said, I shall see that your physical comforts are well taken care of, Mrs. Wannamaker," the Englishman continued. "Your room is waiting for you. If you like, my housekeeper will provide a bath with hot water from a mineral spring behind the lodge."

Dragoman glanced over his shoulder at Longarm, who was gathering up his gear, which the Indian had set with the luggage at the bottom of the steps. "Are you back there, Deputy Long?"

"I'm coming."

"You look like a man who could use a stiff drink."

"Looks don't lie, sir."

"What about you, Sinner?" Dragoman asked Cynthia, taking his time climbing the steps for Mrs. Wannamaker's sake. The woman was breathing hard and pushing off her knees with every step. Longarm judged from his own quickening heart and straining lungs that the altitude here at the lodge was probably a good ten thousand feet or more.

"A drink?" Cynthia said. "I would *love* a brandy."

"Brandy it is."

"And I'd appreciate it if you'd stop calling me Sinner, Uncle Charles." Cynthia playfully elbowed the man in his ribs. "I'm too old for such a dubious-sounding nomenclature, and what must Mrs. Wannamaker and Deputy Long think of me?"

Dragoman laughed as he and the women gained the top of the porch stairs, and turned to glance at both Longarm and the flushed and gasping Mrs. Wannamaker. "Let me explain. The 'Sinner' nickname is merely short for Cynthia and was given to my dear lovely niece by none other than my daughter Lucy herself when the two girls were too young to be able to communicate properly. Cynthia, in turn, had a handle for Lucy."

"Lulu," Cynthia said, rolling her eyes with chagrin. "What a horror you are, Uncle. I hope this will be the end of the 'little Cynthia' and 'little Lucy' tales. You've already bored my traveling companions to tears, I'm afraid, and"—she elbowed him again, a little harder this time— "you're embarrassing me!"

Dragoman threw his head back and laughed. Looking around, Longarm followed the man and the two women inside.

Dragoman stopped in a great timbered hall that was rife with the smell of pine resin and smoke from a near fire, and bellowed, "Sumah!"

The echo of his call hadn't died before a slender, dark-haired woman appeared like a ghost in one of several doorways opening off the foyer. She was dressed in a cream housedress and apron, but her features were every bit as Indian as those of the man who'd piloted the coach.

"Ah," said Dragoman. "I tell you, sometimes I think

this woman knows what's in my head before I do. Cynthia, Marshal, Mrs. Wannamaker, this is Wolf's sister, Sumah. She'll take care of all your needs while you're here. Baths, towels, food, drink—she'll either bring it or send her brother."

A faint smile quirked the Indian woman's mouth, but she kept her chocolate eyes on the floor, her work-roughened hands entwined at her waist.

"For right now, Sumah, please escort Mrs. Wannamaker to that big room on the second floor, just down the hall from the stairs. Two fireplaces in that one, and a big comfortable bed."

When Sumah had led Mrs. Wannamaker up the massive stairs at the far end of the foyer, Dragoman hooked his arm, and Cynthia poked her own through it as he indicated the large doorway on the foyer's right side. "Now, for a drink—shall we? I'm well stocked for living so remote. Right in here, please, Deputy Long. You can leave your rifle and saddlebags on the floor there. Wolf will be along soon, and take them up to your room."

Longarm looked around, hesitating. He set his saddlebags down, then leaned his rifle against the wall, over the bags.

Dragoman and Cynthia had stopped just inside the doorway, both looking back at him. "Ah, a man joined at the hip with his rifle. I can understand that, Marshal Long. Bring it on here with you, if you wish."

"That's all right. Just a habit. I'm sure it'll be fine here in the hall."

"I'm rather close to my own shootin' irons," Dragoman said as he led Cynthia on into what appeared a large parlor with a fire snapping and popping in a wagon-sized, fieldstone hearth. "Of course, I only use mine for hunting animals. You, on the other hand, use yours for hunting men—the most cunning prey of all."

"I reckon you could say that," Longarm allowed, doffing his hat as he entered the parlor—a room with as many square feet as many houses he'd been in, and filled with large wood and leather furniture, with game trophies and hides adorning the walls.

What caught the brunt of Longarm's attention, however, was the gun case on the wall opposite the fireplace. There must have been a good thirty rifles in there, with pistols adorning the bottom shelf. They were shooting irons of nearly every make and model that Longarm had ever heard of and many he hadn't. Beside the gun rack was a crossbow of what appeared varnished ash strapped with sun-cured rawhide and armed with a red-fletched bow with a polished steel tip that fairly glowed in the firelight.

Longarm whistled and planted his hands on his hips, inspecting the well-cared-for weapons racked before him, near a wooden dummy bedecked with German siege armor that likely dated back to the thirteenth or fourteenth century.

"Impressive, eh, Deputy?"

"Just a mite."

Dragoman laughed. "I'll introduce you to some of my friends later. For now, please sit." Dragoman headed for a massive oak cabinet, opening the top drawers to an array of bottles and decanters and demijohns attesting to the notion that the man was nearly as fond of spirits as he was of weaponry.

"Brandy for my niece," the man said. "For you, Marshal Long?"

"Maryland rye, if you have it."

"Ahh," Dragoman said, obviously impressed by the choice. "I see you're a man who appreciates liquor as well as guns."

"Fortunately. I'd feel sort of out of place here if I didn't."

Cynthia had taken a seat on one of the two overstuffed leather couches facing each other in front of the fire. Longarm's glance met hers briefly as he was deciding where he should sit, then, responding to her unspoken command, let his lean frame sag down into the couch right across from her.

"Where's Lucy?" Cynthia inquired as Dragoman splashed brandy into a glass. "When will she be joining—?"

She was interrupted by an ear-rattling shriek punctuated with, "Not only will she be joining you, you old sinner, but she already has!"

Longarm turned to see a blond girl about the same age and build as Cynthia come storming into the parlor wearing a black leather skirt and an untucked hickory blouse with a pearl necklace, long diamond earrings hanging from her ears.

"Lucy!" Cynthia exclaimed, bolting to her feet and running to meet her cousin halfway between the door and the couch.

When they'd finished hugging and pecking each other's cheeks and muttering a long, intimate welcome, Cynthia turned her cousin around to face Longarm. It was like getting hit in the chest with a Sioux war hatchet.

For the woman Longarm was looking at could have been Cynthia's blond, hazel-eyed twin. Which meant she was one of the two most beautiful women he'd ever seen.

# Chapter 9

Hazel eyes leaning toward green set in ever so slightly slanted sockets. Gold-blond hair framing an oval-shaped faced molded to high-cheeked perfection. Lips long and rich and the color of polished rubies.

A figure every bit as ripe and man torturing as the one her cousin, Cynthia, sported.

The long-fingered hand she extended to Longarm was pale and as perfect as the rest of her, with a nondescript silver ring adorning only its middle finger. "Pleased to make your acquaintance, Marshal Long. My, you are tall, aren't you?"

"The pleasure is mine," Longarm said, squeezing the girl's hand in his.

"How did you ever land the luxurious job of escorting my dear cousin into the high Colorado wilds?" Lucy Dragoman boldly shepherded her gaze up and down Longarm's brawny frame, letting it caress the gun holstered on his left hip for nearly as long as it pondered the breadth of his shoulders drawing his frock coat taut across his chest.

"I would think they'd need a man like you out hunting killers or highwaymen . . ." She dropped her chin slightly and a faint mischief sparkled in her eyes.

She was like her cousin in more ways than in just the beauty department, the lawdog thought, trying to imagine how she'd look nude.

"Longarm here is being rewarded for several jobs well done," Cynthia said, crossing her arms on her breasts and giving the lawman a wistful, faintly teasing, more-than-a-little-admiring look, much like that of her cousin's. "Isn't that right, Marshal?"

Longarm shifted his boots uncomfortably on the deep Oriental throw rug beneath him. "And a more than adequate reward I've never known, Miss Larimer."

"Oh, come now," Lucy admonished, switching her gaze between them now. "Why so formal, Marshal Long? You and my cousin certainly must mean more to each other than *official business*. Look at the both of you—why, what a handsome pair!"

"Now, Lucy," Charles Dragoman interjected, "can't you see you're embarrassing the both of them? That's no way to treat guests of Dragoman Lodge."

"Oh, yes," Cynthia said, gently chiding her uncle and adeptly changing the subject, "you would certainly never try to embarrass me—now, would you, Uncle Charles?"

Dragoman chuckled. "A drink, daughter?"

"Oh, later, Poppa," Lucy said, suddenly bouncing girlishly up and down on her toes and turning to Cynthia, taking both her cousin's hands in her own. "Come along, cousin—won't you? I've much to show you around the place. Oh, you're going to love it here, and I just know you're going to want to extend your trip when you see the horses and the riding trails!"

Cynthia looked from Longarm to Charles Dragoman, as if requesting permission to be excused.

"Off with the both of you," Dragoman intoned with mock severity. "I've been wanting to show the lawman my weapons, anyway, and break out the Cuban cigars! Just don't wander too far. McCallum will likely be serving up the elk haunch in an hour or so."

"Come, Cynthia," Lucy said, grabbing her cousin's arm.

Cynthia's eyes were on Longarm, at once beseeching and apologetic. He responded with a smile and a furtive little wave of his fingers. He really didn't mind her leaving him here in the company of Dragoman, who was proving to be a most interesting host. And he wouldn't mind a cigar. Besides, Cynthia hadn't seen Lucy in years, and they naturally had much catching up to do.

When the women had left, Dragoman refreshed his and Longarm's drinks and broke open a humidor of Cuban cigars that he got fresh, he said, twice a year by special order from Florida. Then, both men puffing and drinking, Dragoman opened his gun cabinet and gave Longarm a detailed showing of his weaponry—an arsenal so varied and rare that Longarm's lower jaw was soon hanging down around the ends of his string tie.

He was shown guns and knives from around the world and all along the centuries, including Italian flintlock sporting guns dating from around 1680, an engraved Indian tulwar from the sixth century, a dagger from central Asia, and a rare Custer Range Springfield M1873 Trapdoor carbine. In a special trophy room off the parlor, the Englishman turned American frontiersman showed Longarm his favorite relic of all—a perfectly preserved set of Japanese samurai armor complete with cherry-handled sword.

Longarm was mesmerized. There was nothing like inspecting relics, especially war relics, to give one a sense of mankind's tumultuous and colorful history, no less magically engrossing for being so savage. Men were never so inventive as when they were trying to kill each other. When Dragoman had finished showing him a Spanish military *carabineros* drum and had tossed another log on the fire, they returned to their respective couches in front of the hearth.

Dragoman splashed more rye into Longarm's goblet and more Russian brandy into his own. "So, Marshal, if you'll forgive me for asking, how many men have you put away or caused to be hanged?"

The question, asked so frankly and with Dragoman's gray eyes boring into his own, with that hideous scar running down through the right unmoored one, took Longarm aback.

"Oh . . . too many to count, I reckon. I got into the racket some time ago, Mr. Dragoman."

"Call me Charles. And might I—?"

"My friends call me Longarm."

Dragoman gave a hearty chuckle as he adjusted his position in the deep leather couch. "The long arm of the law. I like that. You must be quite effective at your job, Longarm."

"I leave the assessments of my abilities up to my boss."

Dragoman seemed to like that, too, as he stared at the lawman with a thoughtful admiration slightly furrowing his silver-gray brows. "How many planted in boneyards?"

Longarm had just sipped his drink, and now over the brim of his well-filled glass, he croaked, "Say again?"

"How many have you kicked out with a shovel, Longarm? Come on, now, my good man. Don't be coy!"

It was Longarm's turn to laugh. He did so a mite uncomfortably and returned the man's probing stare. "I don't
know."

"Too many to count?"

"I don't know if it's that exactly, though I reckon there
have been quite a few. It's just not something I reckon I'd
want to keep track of. Hunting lawless men is my job, Mr.
Dragoman . . . uh, Charles . . . but the killing is no special
treat. In fact, it's one of the job's nasty by-products, one I
don't like to think about too often."

"Does it disgust you?"

"I reckon you could say that. Makes me feel right
nasty, even when I've taken down a man who needed takin'
down. You always know you're killin' a human bein',
that's all." He shrugged and took a deep puff off his cigar.

Dragoman arched a brow and stared at Longarm even
more intently. "Are you telling me that hunting men has
never given you a surge of excitement, Longarm?"

"In the heat of the moment, maybe." The lawman felt
himself growing uncomfortable—why, he wasn't sure.
"But when I track a man, my aim isn't to kill him. It's to
bring him to justice, to a judge and a jury. When I can't do
that, when I've had to kill that man, I've failed."

"Right professional attitude, Marshal." Dragoman held
up his glass in salute and drank.

"Ah, hell," Longarm said, thinking about it though it
felt like a can of worms he'd as soon remained sealed. "I
reckon most of that was true. On the other hand, I have to
admit that when the chips are down, a surge of excitement
does tend to take over. The thrill of the kill, no matter how
barbaric. Probably left over from our caveman days. I
suppose, since I've been drinking your fine rye, I might as
well own up to that feeling now and then, probably some-

thing akin to what you felt bringin' down that big bruin yonder."

Longarm held up his own glass to indicate the giant grizzly head over the fireplace. It was a wonderfully preserved trophy, eyes black and malevolent, long yellow teeth bared in the fury at the heart of a savage battle.

Dragoman pondered the bruin for a time, absently turning his glass in his big, calloused hand. "Oh, yes. I felt all of that and more. The fear that comes when you think you've taken your last breath, your last sip of a good drink, loved your last woman. Didn't even know I'd killed the beast and that it hadn't killed me until I awakened in my room upstairs."

The Englishman sipped his drink and winced a little at the burn of the brandy in his throat, keeping his thoughtful gaze directed at the bear. "My son and several of our hands told me they found us together, the bear and me, entangled like lovers who'd killed themselves copulating."

He chuckled, obviously delighted at the idea of this.

"Blood everywhere. My Swiss Bruelmann rifle lay nearby, empty. As did my Colt pistol. I had two big bowie knifes clutched in my hands so tightly they had to pry each finger from their handles one at a time, and roll me gently out from under the magnificent thing. He'd fallen on my leg, which was broken in three places. Every rib was broken, my left shoulder was dislocated, my left wrist was shattered, and my face, as you can see, was cut to ribbons."

"But you made it."

"I did indeed. And except for the eye, I'm better than ever." Dragoman slapped the couch beside him and bunched his lips and narrowed his eyes defiantly at Longarm. "Tougher and meaner, and if such an animal ever shows himself again in these mountains, I'll be ready for him. May the better beast win!"

Longarm couldn't help smiling at this, but he felt a little wary, as well. In the back of his brain he couldn't help feeling that maybe Dragoman hadn't really completely recovered from his fight with the griz.

"This is a vast, remote range," the lawman said, making conversation. "Surely there's more grizzlies like him. Maybe even bigger."

"Not around here." Dragoman shook his head regretfully. "I've been here damn near twenty years now—I came several years before I brought Lucy and Bentley, to build the place and set things in order. Between me and the men who've worked for me, we've pretty much shot or scared off all the real game. Oh, you'll find a few deer now and then, even some elk. But no bears or mountain lions or even wolves unless I bait them in. Nothing that gets your blood up to hunt it. Nothing like him."

Dragoman lifted his glass to indicate the bear once more, to salute the beast that had nearly killed him. He sipped from the glass.

Longarm leaned forward to tap ashes from his cigar into a carved wooden ashtray on the table between the sofas. "I thought I smelled a forgotten game cache as we were driving up the canyon. Might that have been grizzly bait?"

Dragoman slid his gaze quickly back toward Longarm again, and there was a funny little tightening of the skin around the man's mouth, and a slight darkening of both eyes. "Oh," he said. "Yes, that's probably what it was. I had my men set out a stillborn foal several days ago. I've heard a family of bears has been wandering the next watershed to the west, and I thought I might be able to bait the bull in. Magnificent creatures. Deadly when they're threatened. A real challenge to kill. If he comes over here, I'll go out with my Bruelmann again"—he held up his hand that held his cigar and peeled his index finger away from the stogie—"but with only one bullet. And one bowie."

He winked and threw back the last of his drink.

"Get a little bored out here, do you, Charles?" Longarm said, trying to add a little levity to the conversation that had suddenly become a little maudlin, to his taste.

"Bored? Hell, no. I have a small mining interest to the east, and I ride over there three times a week to look over the books. We're trying to get a small-gauge rail line laid, to haul the ore out for processing, as processing it on site has become less cost-effective than when we were first starting out. And . . ."

Dragoman let his voice trail off, and then he flushed a little—a boyish expression of chagrin.

"Ah, hell, Longarm. You came clean, so I reckon I will, as well. You're right. I do get a little bored now and then. Fortunately, however, I have my daughter, who's a magnificent chess player and whose conversation is always inspiring and thought-provoking, and my son, who keeps me in the saddle and riding about the mountains looking for new sources of game. We'll be taking one such ride first thing in the morning. Bentley and I and a couple of our men. Are you up for it?"

"I don't know," Longarm said, his thoughts turning to Cynthia. He didn't mind a ride to get the lay of the mountains out here, but he'd sort of had his own sights set on another kind of ride, not to mention another kind of lay. "I, uh . . ."

"Oh, of course, you will," Dragoman intoned, sounding a little drunk all of a sudden. "I'll have our best horse saddled and waiting for you at six, after a hearty breakfast!"

"In the meantime, Poppa," came a female's raspy, sexy voice from the doorway, "Mr. McCallum has informed me that dinner will be served in five minutes."

Longarm turned to the parlor door to see Miss Lucy Dragoman smiling in at him from the hall. The blond was resplendent in a ruby red silk gown and long, pearl earrings. Her hair hung loose, with ringlets arranged over her china white ears. Her lace-edged bodice was cut so low that Longarm's throat swelled. It must have shown in his face.

The girl's crystalline eyes sparkled as she blushed. Her bosom heaved as she turned and drifted away like a haunting but dissipating dream.

The smell of cherry blossoms lingered—nearly the same smell that accompanied the girl's raven-haired cousin— and Longarm felt his underwear tighten across his crotch.

"Shall we, Longarm?" Dragoman said, setting his glass down and gaining his feet with a grunt. "I'm so hungry I could eat two of those damn bruins." He slapped Longarm heartily on the back. "Oh, you're gonna have a fine time here. I just know it!"

# Chapter 10

Looking across the table at the two beautiful women seated across from him at the dining table of Dragoman Lodge was like having an especially stout Apache warrior punch a hole in Longarm's chest, then reach in and squeeze his heart while twisting it counterclockwise. Cynthia and her cousin, Miss Lucy Dragoman, were truly living jewels.

And Longarm didn't mind at all that the gowns they each wore were so low-cut as to reveal all but the nipples of their opulent breasts, shoved up and secured by tight bodices. They were so tightly packed into their confines that Longarm could see the veins showing through the pale skin at the tops of all four.

As though to confirm he really wasn't dreaming the visions before him, the supercilious, cow-faced Mrs. Wannamaker sat to Longarm's right, just around the corner from Charles Dragoman, whose ears she talked off as she ate, assuring the man that her taste was impeccable and that she was thoroughly capable of enjoying the elk haunch that the man's cook—a burly, moody Scot named

McCallum—had roasted in wild onions, black pepper, and a sauce made from lemons and chokecherries. The wine that Dragoman served with the meal had lifted a flush in the woman's fat cheeks, and put a slight tremble into her oddly smooth and high-pitched voice, raising it another grating notch.

That was it for the diners, though to Longarm's left at the heavy timbered, white-clothed table that was large enough for a dinner party twice again the current one's size, was an unused place setting. The plate and wineglass had been placed there, Dragoman had explained when they'd all first been seated, in the event his son, "who fancied himself a cardsharp, could pull himself away from the hired men's bunkhouse long enough to grace them with his presence."

That hadn't happened yet, and Longarm had a feeling it wouldn't. Maybe the young Dragoman had spied Mrs. Wannamaker waddling her way into the dining room and decided that poker in the hired men's bunkhouse would be a more desirable way to spend the evening.

"So, Marshal Long," said Lucy Dragoman, looking across the table at him from beneath her thin, sandy brows, "Cynthia tells me that you're quite a noted law bringer around the West. Do you enjoy your work?"

The cook had just cleared away the main course leavings and set out a big bowl of bread pudding with a bottle of cognac before limping, customarily taciturn, back to his kitchen.

Longarm glanced at Cynthia. "When my assignments are as much fun as this one . . . and I'm served good vittles like these . . . how could I possibly say I didn't?"

"Perhaps you would join Cynthia and me and Mrs.

Wannamaker, of course, in the parlor for an after-dinner drink? And you could relate a few stories? I don't get out of these mountains much, I'm afraid." Lucy slid her lightly admonishing gaze to Dragoman. "But I'd love to hear what goes on in the exciting and, I'm sure, rather violent world of a deputy United States marshal."

"Oh, good heavens!" gasped Mrs. Wannamaker. "Such stories as those told by a man like . . . well, of Marshal Long's ilk . . . certainly wouldn't be appropriate for the ears of young ladies. I don't mean to be presumptuous, of course, Miss Dragoman, but being the elder female at the table I feel it's my duty to voice good sense and to tout accepted manners. Even out here in the Colorado wild!"

Cynthia dropped her eyes to her plate in embarrassment. Lucy Dragoman stared at her cousin's chaperone for a time, as though she hadn't understood what the woman had said. Dragoman himself gave the woman a faintly tolerant, bemused study, and then, dropping his fork on his empty dessert plate, raked a red paw down his scarred face and yawned.

"Well, I'm afraid I'll have to let you three work out the finer points of civility on your own. I'm an early-to-bed man. Early to bed, early to rise, and all that rot." Dragoman stood and bowed to his niece. "Cynthia, thank you for the privilege of seeing your lovely visage once again. Mrs. Wannamaker, it's been a pleasure. Marshal, please don't forget our bright and early excursion. Shall I have McCallum wake you at five?"

"I'll make it. Thanks for supper."

"The pleasure was mine."

Dragoman kissed each of the girls, gave Mrs. Wannamaker a nod, and took his leave.

"Well, it was a long trip," Longarm said, rising from his chair and tossing his napkin onto his plate. "I reckon I'll be heading to bed myself."

"I'll have Wolf show you." Lucy called to the big Indian, who was apparently helping the cook in the kitchen, then returned her gaze to Longarm. "Please enjoy a hot bath, Marshal Long. I'll instruct Wolf to haul up water from the natural hot spring beneath the house. My father's design."

"That'd suit me just fine, Miss Dragoman." Longarm nodded at Cynthia. "Miss Larimer, your bodyguard is retiring. He'll see you in the morning."

He couldn't keep a slight ironic edge out of his voice though his smile was fixed as he turned from the girls to Mrs. Wannamaker with a courtly bow. As Wolf entered the dining room, drying his ham-sized hands on a white towel, Lucy instructed him to provide Longarm with a bath. The sexually frustrated lawman headed on out of the dining room and toward the massive stairs while Wolf clomped along behind him.

The Indian led the lawman up to the second story by way of camphene bracket lamps and down a narrow hall paneled in split pine logs. Wolf opened a timbered door in which a lamp already burned, and a fire glowed in a fieldstone hearth in the room's left wall, opposite the quilt-covered bed on the right. A simple room but cozily furnished with yet more buckhorns and hides on the walls. A bearskin rug lay on the floor beside the bed, the head still attached.

As Wolf began to stir the fire's ashes with an iron poker, Longarm walked to the room's single dormer window and looked out. The sun was down but a faint afterglow lit the stony wall of the mountain behind the lodge. The ground dropped between the lodge and the mountain, carpeted in pines, and Longarm could make out the roofs of outbuildings farther down the hill, nearer the mountain wall.

He tossed his hat on a chair and, working the knot out of his string tie, he started to turn away from the window. He stopped suddenly, frowning, and turned back. Movement had caught his eye.

Now as he stared down through the dark pines he saw three horseback riders moving at a slant from right to left down the grade behind the lodge. They were dressed in fur coats, collars raised against the chill, high-country night. One rider was dragging something about six feet behind his black, white-stockinged horse. It appeared an oblong, dark bundle. Longarm couldn't see it nor the riders clearly because of the rocks and trees, and then the riders dropped down the grade and out of sight.

Hunters, most likely. They must have found something to shoot out here despite what Dragoman had said about the game being scarce. That bundle hadn't looked like a log they were dragging back to be cut up into stove wood. Longarm almost asked Wolf about the riders, but then he remembered the savage scar across the man's throat.

When Wolf had stoked the fire and produced a copper bathing tub from a closet down the hall, and set it in front of the fire before leaving the room again in his silent, heavy-footed way, Longarm sagged into an upholstered chair by the window. He kicked out of his boots and lit a three-for-a-nickel cheroot.

He was tired after the long ride. Bone-tired. He enjoyed being with Cynthia, and he'd even enjoyed meeting the quirky, reclusive, gun-crazy Dragoman, but the trip would be a whole lot more like a vacation if Mrs. Wannamaker hadn't been ridin' Cynthia's heels and keeping Longarm from getting his dong wet.

When Wolf had returned with two buckets of steaming, briny-smelling water and filled the tub, Longarm shucked out of his clothes and sank down in the hot, sulfurous water for a good, long soak. He lay his head back against the tub and slowly smoked his cheroot.

But he couldn't fully relax. Why did those men he'd seen riding behind the lodge keep dancing around behind his eyelids? Just his lawman's snoot always sniffing around for trouble, he reckoned.

He closed his eyes, rolled the cheroot to one corner of his mouth, and let his muscles relax in the soothingly hot water.

Someone tapped on his door. He jerked his head up, and the cheroot dropped into the tub with a sizzle. His first instinct was to reach for his .44-40, but then as the sleep fog lifted from his brain, he remembered where he was.

Out in the middle of nowhere, amongst friends.

"Who is it?"

There were three more, softer taps on his door. Then the latch clicked, the door came open suddenly, and none other than Cynthia herself slipped through the gap. Turning quickly, she closed the door, wincing as she let the latching bolt click back into place.

She turned to him, long hair dancing, her skirts swishing about her long legs.

"You're overdressed," Longarm said.

"*Shhhh!*" Cynthia pressed two fingers to her lips. "Mrs. Wannamaker is on the other end of the hall, and I think she suspects that you and I are concocting a tryst."

"Hell," Longarm growled, sitting back in the tub and letting his gaze run down the black-haired beauty's cool, slim, high-busted figure. "I think we done got one at long last. Shuck out of them duds and climb in here, girl." He grinned as he poked the soggy cheroot between his lips. "I'll wash your back if you wash mine."

"Custis, will you please keep your voice down?"

"If I talk any quieter," he rasped, "I won't be sayin' anything at all."

As she walked toward him with a faint, beguiling smile pulling the corners of her rich mouth up, Longarm pushed himself up out of the water to a standing position. "Here, let me help."

"I can't climb in there," she whispered, stopping a foot away from him.

Immediately working at the buttons of her gown's tight bodice, Longarm said, "What do you mean you can't climb in here? Sharing a bath has sorta become a tradition with us."

"We'll make too much noise."

"We'll go slow and easy."

Cynthia laughed with delight, then clapped her hands over her mouth. "Don't say things like that, you bruin!"

"Don't be a chickenshit, for chrissakes, Cynthia. That old hag is probably dead asleep already. Shit, she had two glasses of wine and I can tell she can't hold it any better than a minister's wife. Besides, it was a long trip. She's out, I tell you. Now climb in here, and let's go for a ride!"

She pulled back away from him, a sultry, faintly teasing expression making her face sparkle. As she swung wide of the tub, just beyond his reach, she continued to unbutton her dress and slide the sleeves halfway down her arms, so that the bodice dropped to just beneath her nipples yet still pushing those delightful orbs up high and full, like baby pumpkins.

"I have a better idea. That tub's a little small, and Mrs. Wannamaker will probably hear the water splashing, not to mention my scream when you assault me with that club of yours." Cynthia dropped her eyes to the organ in question, which was already at nearly full mast though she'd been in the room only a minute.

Longarm's voice was so thick he had to clear it before he rasped, "What's the idea? Not that it matters. I reckon I'm open to anything." His eyes were glued to her budlike nipples.

"You'll see."

She slowly stripped for him, blue eyes glued to his. When she was down to her camisole and pantaloons, she sat in a chair, and his cock grew harder and harder as, with excruciating slowness, she removed her stockings and garter belt.

Then the pantaloons came off just as slowly, exposing her long, china-white legs with delicate, tender white feet. She spread her legs slightly as she stood up from the chair, giving a glimpse of her black-haired snatch and an even more enticing, even briefer glimpse of the tantalizing pink folds amongst the silky fur at her crotch.

"Climb on out of there," she whispered huskily, letting her tongue work her lower lip over alluringly as she dropped her smoky eyes to his cock. "And I'll let you take off the rest."

Longarm lifted one leg too quickly. Water splashed. Cynthia shushed him angrily though the anger didn't reach her lust-bright eyes. Slowly, he lifted the other leg out of the tub and strode across the wood floor to her. She handed him a towel off the chair, and he dried off, breath-

ing hard as his eyes remained stuck on her, riveted, while
her own eyes slid across his brawny bulk slowly, dropping
every now and then to his raging hard-on and widening
with fascination and expectation.

He threw the towel on the chair, then lifted her camisole up and over her head. Her hair fluttered back over her
shoulders and down her chest. Longarm slid the thick
locks away from her breasts, then lowered his head to
nuzzle the valley between them.

As he did, she stepped in closer to him, giving little
sighs of passion, and wrapped a warm, soft hand around
his cock and gave him a slightly less-than-gentle squeeze.
She pumped him as he nuzzled, then licked her breasts,
raking his mustache lightly across her nipples. She always
liked having his mustache on her nipples, and he watched
with a grin now as they both pebbled and stood up at attention, becoming as round and firm as spring rosebuds.

"I didn't think we'd ever get this far," Longarm whispered in her ear as he nibbled her lobe.

She was rubbing her hand hungrily up and down his
cock, and moaning faintly, her breasts rising and falling as
her breathing became shallow and labored.

"Be prepared to stop at a moment's notice," she said,
pumping him harder. "Like I said, I think she's onto us,
and . . . I wouldn't . . . want . . . Aunt May or . . . Uncle
William . . ."

She couldn't continue, because just then he turned her
around to face the bed, and she dropped forward, hands
on the edge of the bed as he spread her legs with his
knees.

"You surprise me, Miss Larimer," Longarm growled,
his own breaths coming short and his heart shuddering
against his breastbone. "Are you the one who blew me

under your dear uncle's desk during the Larimer Christmas ball?"

She gave a husky, restrained giggle. "I did do that, didn't I?"

"You sure did."

He nudged the mushroom end of his swollen, red cock up under her ass and against the swollen, furred mound of her snatch. She lifted her head suddenly and tensed her entire body. "Never tasted anything so good in my life, if you want to know the truth about it. Not . . . that . . . I"—he was sliding his cock inside her—"hadn't blown you . . . before . . . but for some reason . . . you tasted— uhh, *gawwwd*!"

"Shhhh!"

"See—I told you this would happen," she snarled as he fucked her.

"It's your fault." Longarm rammed his cock deep inside her and then pulled slowly out as he reached around her to squeeze her breasts and to roll her ever-hardening and jutting nipples between his fingers. "I was just takin' a bath and gettin' ready to climb into my pajamas—*whew!* That was a good one!—before you rapped on my door, lookin' for love."

"Shut up and fuck me."

"Like a damn alley cat in heat is what you are, Miss Larimer."

"Oh, Jesus . . . when you go slow like this . . . I swear . . . my . . . heart's . . . going to *explode*!"

"Shhh!"

"Oh, damn you, Custis!"

Longarm held her tighter and increased his pace, curling his toes into the bear rug and hammering his hips forward. He was pounding her so hard a few minutes later that the bed began barking against the wall. Grabbing her around the waist and holding himself deep inside her, he eased her down to the bear rug and finished her there.

Hard.

When he finally pulled his dwindling cock out of her she was chewing her hand to keep from screaming. Her hair was wonderfully disheveled about her crimson face and chafed breasts and on the bear rug beneath her. Her hair and the bear's were almost exactly the same color.

Longarm sat down on the edge of the bed, breathless, and lay back. He could hear Cynthia breathing on the rug. Her breath slowed gradually.

"Whew!" The beauty rose slowly, looked sidelong up at Longarm, then reached into the tub. She pulled out the dripping sponge and wriggled on her naked ass over to him and began slowly, gently cleaning his cock that had fallen back across his left hip like the head of a slumbering goose.

Longarm smiled at the girl's soft and gentle ministrations.

"Such a wonderful organ," she said a tad more loudly than they'd been speaking before. If Mrs. Wannamaker hadn't heard the previous commotion, she was dead asleep.

"Yours ain't so bad theirselves."

"Whoops. Uh-oh. This one is coming alive again."

Again, Longarm smiled, keeping his eyes closed, nearly hypnotized by the girl's warm fingers and the wet sponge. He lay there in total bliss, feeling his nerve endings prickling once more until he also felt his loins swell and the head of his cock rise from his belly like an awakening sidewinder.

Something more wet and more warm and wielding

touched the underside of his shaft just down from its head. It was like an electric shock firing through his entire body. His legs tensed. He looked down to see the top of Cynthia's head moving slowly from side to side and up and down. Her hair screened her face, but through a few thin strands he saw the tip of her tongue sliding slowly down his length to its base and then back up again to the tip. She opened her mouth wider and dropped it over the end of him, her pink lips bulging out around it, her tongue lapping him delightfully.

Longarm dug his fists into the bed. "Jesus."

She looked up at him, grinning. "Did you miss me?"

"I figured you'd gotten tired of old Custis, flown the proverbial coup. Maybe even got hitched to a count or some such."

Cynthia smiled, eyes flashing with delight at his obvious jealousy. "Nope. Just busy in Paris, helping a friend from the Sorbonne get his work shown around town." She lowered her head and sucked Longarm like a lollipop before lifting her head again.

"I was thinking of you, though. Thought of writing you, but knowing how you're always gallivanting around the frontier, riding and shooting and fucking and God knows what else, I figured you'd never read my letters before I could make it back to you myself."

Longarm grunted as she lowered her tongue to his scrotum.

"Are you having a good time?" she asked, her eyes suddenly serious, a slight pout on her wet lips. A tiny string of saliva hung between her lower lip and the tip of his swollen organ.                    .

Longarm chuckled and dropped his head back down on the bed. "Your chaperone aside, I'm doin' all right. It ain't Dodge City or Fort Worth, but as long as we can sneak away together a time or two . . ."

"That's a wonderful answer. And for that you will be amply rewarded, my well-endowed lawdog."

She lowered her head and performed on him the longest, most excruciating fellatio that he'd ever experienced. And he'd experienced a few blow jobs in his time—a good many provided by Cynthia's own sweet lips and tongue, in fact. When she'd finished and his heart had started beating again, she licked him clean, using one hand to tilt his dwindling hard-on every which way so she didn't miss a drop.

She'd just deemed him clean as a parson's front window when someone tapped on the door.

"Cynthia?" Though she kept her voice low, Mrs. Wannamaker sounded suspicious. "Are you in there, dear?"

# Chapter 11

Cynthia clapped her hands over her mouth to cover a gasp. Her naked breasts curved down beneath her elbows.

Longarm sat up, placed his hands on the girl's shoulders, and gently turned her aside as he rose, then pulled the naked beauty to her feet and just as gently shoved her back behind the dresser, out of sight from the door. Cynthia's cobalt blue eyes were large as 'dobe dollars. She held her laced hands beneath her chin, elbows pressed against her breasts.

Longarm grabbed his hat off the dresser, set it on his head, canting it at a rakish angle, and whispered, "Let me handle this."

*"Custis!"* she rasped as, naked except for the hat, cock swinging like a railroad signal flag, Longarm sauntered over to the door.

He tipped his head to the timbered panel. "Can I help you, Mrs. Wannamaker?"

The woman said quietly but shrilly, "Is Miss Larimer in there?"

Cynthia gasped again as Longarm, gesturing for her to stay where she was with one hand, opened the door with the other. He drew it half open and filled it with his six-foot-plus, broad, naked bulk, leaning one shoulder against the side of the door, the other against the door frame.

Mrs. Wannamaker stood in the hall, two feet away from Longarm. She stared up at him, mouth agape.

"Now, what would a nice young lady like Miss Larimer possibly be doing in the room of a man simply enjoying a long, leisurely bath?"

The woman's jowls quivered. The blood left her lips and slid up into her fleshy cheeks as she let her wide, exasperated eyes travel the length of Longarm's big, thick, scarred, buck-naked body from his face, which towered above hers, to his crotch. As though slapped, she leaped straight back in the hall and sort of mewled, moving her mouth like a fish.

"Oh, my *gawd*!"

Cowering like a dog and covering her eyes with one hand, the woman, clad in a long flannel nightgown and holding a lantern in her other hand, wheeled quickly and fairly ran back to a door standing open on the other end of the hall. She scampered inside, cast a quick glance at Longarm once more, then shrieked, *"Ohhhh!"* and slammed the door closed.

Longarm closed his own door and turned to Cynthia, who'd slumped to the floor and sat on her rump, laughing hysterically into her hands, tears streaming down her cheeks.

"Custis," she chastised him finally, whispering. "You might've given her a heart stroke!"

In case Mrs. Wannamaker came looking for her incorrigible charge once again, Cynthia grabbed her clothes, gave

Longarm a lusty parting kiss, nibbling his lower lip and fingering his dong, then ran out the door and down the carpeted hall toward her own room. Longarm stood in the doorway, watching her bare, round ass. Aware of his leer, she poked her head out her door, blew him a kiss and a parting grin, then lightly closed her door.

Longarm retreated into his own digs, which seemed especially lonely now after the saucy coupling with his favorite debutante. He crawled into the comfortable bed, trying to relax his muscles as well as his mind, but still, for some reason he couldn't sleep. He felt as though he'd guzzled a pot of coffee only a half hour ago.

He lay back, frowning up at the dark ceiling, probing his unconscious. It didn't take much digging before he realized what was nettling him. The men he'd seen earlier, dragging the curious object through the trees behind the lodge.

"Go to sleep," he told himself aloud. "You're on vacation. Billy said so himself."

But he'd been a lawman too long to set the remembered image aside. The timeworn urge to investigate kept prodding his brain until, finally, with a frustrated sigh he tossed the covers aside and climbed out of bed.

"Okay, damnit, let's go have a look." He lit the gas lamp on the dresser. "Just remember," he added, grumbling to himself, "you're a guest here. Don't offend anybody or embarrass yourself. Not that you haven't done both before, but this is Cynthia's party, and you don't want her mad at you."

He chuckled at that. No man in his mind would want to get crossways with Cynthia and have the plug pulled on nights like the one he'd just spent—one as close to heaven as any man with his checkered past was ever going to get.

Ten minutes later, he'd stumbled through the lodge and somehow in the misty darkness relieved only by ambient light from the windows, found a back door. It was off a storeroom that smelled of molasses and cured meat. The hinges squawked as he flipped up the metal latch and pushed it open. He winced, opened the door more slowly, and stepped out through a three-foot gap.

When he'd closed the door, he turned to face the lodge's backyard, and turned up the collar of his frock coat against the high-country chill. It might have still been summer in Denver, but up here it was nearly autumn. Snow would be falling soon, probably piling up as high as the door and staying there till late April or early May.

Crazy damn country to remain in all year round. Men went mad up here of a winter.

Longarm took a deep, intoxicating draught of the piney tang. Faintly, he could smell horses and hay. The barns were down the grade, near the base of the mountain wall that rose up before him, as dark as a massive black velvet curtain. The men he'd seen earlier must have been heading toward them.

It was dark out here, but as Longarm's eyes adjusted, he realized it wasn't as dark as he'd thought. There was plenty of starlight, and a milky wash in the sky told him the moon must have been rising somewhere on the lodge's other side, quartering over its eastern end.

Longarm dug a cheroot out of his shirt pocket and stuck it in his mouth but didn't light it. He didn't want to think of himself as skulking around, but he didn't really want anyone to know he was out here, either. More of a quiet, wool-gathering walk, an insomnia-relieving stroll. At least, that's what he'd tell anyone who happened to run into him.

He stepped off the small back porch, walking on the balls of his boots, then continued out into the yard. There were two large stacks of split wood covered with tarps weighted down with dangling logs. More wood hunkered under a stablelike shelter. There was a two-hole privy right of the woodpiles, at the end of a curving brick path.

Beyond the wood was mostly scrub and fir trees with a few aspens. As Longarm made his way down the hill in the darkness, picking his way carefully over the spongy soil, stepping over deadfalls, he glimpsed a trail to his left and angled over to it. The two-track wagon trail curved down the slope and into a shallow canyon, curving around to the left.

Longarm slowed his pace when he saw a few stout log buildings on the floor of the canyon, clumped together under pines and amongst boulders that had long ago fallen from the looming ridge. It was a box canyon, with a wall angling off the high ridge just beyond the buildings, one of which was a square cabin with a shake-shingled roof on which the milky moonlight glistened faintly. The two front windows and the side window facing Longarm were lit. Smoke curled from the stone chimney. A shadow moved behind the front window right of the door.

Directly across the trail from the cabin was a long, L-shaped barn with paddocks behind it and abutting both sides. The horse smell was stronger here.

Longarm continued along the trail, noting the relatively fresh horse tracks and a broad, continuous scuff mark likely made by whatever the men had been dragging. Longarm followed the furrow to a shed sitting about thirty yards from the cabin that was obviously a bunkhouse for Dragoman's hired men. The door to the shed was on the side opposite the cabin, so Longarm didn't hesitate about tripping the latch and walking in. Out of long habit, he stepped quickly to one side, so the door wouldn't back-light him.

Cold and dark in here. Even colder than outside. There was the heady tang of fresh cedar. Frowning, unable to see a thing, Longarm reached into his shirt pocket for a stove match, and fired it on his cartridge belt. He held up the guttering flame. The faint orange glow shoved the dense shadows about ten feet back in a semicircle. It also revealed objects stacked to Longarm's right. Objects covered with wood shavings.

Ice.

Moving slowly forward, the shavings crunching beneath his boots, Longarm held the stove match up higher. On the far wall were shelves, and on the shelves were a variety of root vegetables, squash, pumpkins, and burlap bags spilling potatoes from which long, white ears curled. From the ceiling over Longarm's head, sides of meat hung, including skinned rabbits.

Longarm turned to his left. Just as he glimpsed what appeared a long bundle resting atop the ice, the match burned his fingers. He gave a grunt and dropped it, then reached into his pocket for another.

When he'd fired the lucifer, he held it aloft again and stepped closer to the piled ice bricks. The dancing, orange light skipped and fluttered as it slid over the ice mound, shepherding shadows off the mound's crest, sweeping them back against the log wall where they melted into the ice.

The shadows slid back off the oblong mound, as well, and Longarm frowned when two blue eyes were suddenly staring up at him from a round face capped with a shock of thick, sandy hair.

The man was sprawled on his back atop the stacked ice bricks. There was no blanket over the obviously dead body.

It wore shabby range clothes and a shaggy wolf coat. The coat was open, revealing a nasty gash in his belly from which snakelike intestines curled. A knife wound.

The man had died hard.

Longarm stared at the body for a time, having to light another match, his thoughts turning this way and that. One of Dragoman's men? That slash across his belly had been hand-delivered by a good-sized knife, not an animal's claws.

Murder, then. Would Dragoman report it? Maybe the master of Dragoman lodge didn't know about it yet. Maybe his other men would inform him tomorrow.

Longarm saw no reason to start making inquiries at this late hour though the lights in the bunkhouse told him that some of Dragoman's men were still up. He'd talk to the master of the lodge about the dead man tomorrow. This was not, of course, Longarm's business. Still, he was involved whether he wanted to be or not, whether he was in his jurisdiction or not, and he hoped Dragoman had a reasonable explanation for this gent's death.

Or could get one from his men.

The last thing Longarm wanted to do was get enmeshed in a murder investigation while he was on so-called vacation.

He let his fourth match go out, dropped it on the floor, stepping on it hard to make sure it was out, and started blindly for the door. He put his hand out until he felt the timbers, then dragged his hand down to the latch. Pulling the door inward, he stepped outside and began drawing the door closed behind him.

Something round and hard pressed against the left side of his neck. "One sudden move, amigo, and you're gonna have a mighty large hole in your neck."

The man's voice was low and quiet, teeming with menace. Boots crunched gravel to Longarm's right. Just as he saw the second man in the corner of his right eye, Longarm let his instincts take over. He snapped up his left elbow, slammed it hard against the forearm of the man holding the gun to his neck.

The gun barked loudly in the quiet night, making Longarm's ears ring. The man who'd been holding it cursed as Longarm spun on his left foot and smashed his right fist into the side of the man's head, feeling a wetness against his knuckles.

The man groaned. There was the metallic thud of the gun dropping.

Longarm heard the second man move in quickly behind him. He wheeled, gritting his teeth at the clinking and menacing whir of a chain cutting the air. As he ducked, the chain careened over his head and struck the side of the icehouse with a rattling bark.

Longarm lunged up off his dug-in heels, saw the short, broad figure before him. He was wearing an undershirt, with suspenders holding up baggy trousers. In the darkness, Longarm saw a close-cropped cap of brown curly hair and carefully sculpted muttonchop sideburns. As the man began to recover from his ill-fated attempt to bash Longarm's brains in with the log chain, the lawman drove his left fist into the man's paunch.

The air left the man's lungs with a great *Uhhfff!* of expelled air. He dropped the chain. Lunging forward, Longarm smashed his right knee into the man's face, hearing the sinewy snap of a breaking nose and feeling warm blood seep through his trouser leg.

The man's head snapped up and he stumbled straight backward, throwing his arms out for balance.

Longarm whipped around once more to see the first man bulling toward him, head down, shouting, *"You fuckin' son of a bitch!"*

Longarm tried to sidestep out of the way, but the man was too close, too fast on his feet. He buried his head and right shoulder into Longarm's belly, driving the lawman straight back and lifting him up off his feet.

Longarm hit the ground hard on his back. The stars wheeled as cracked bells tolled in his ears.

Then the first man was on top of him, and Longarm saw the man's right fist careening toward his chin. The lawman snapped his right hand up, his forearm blocking the blow. He wrapped his hand around the man's wrist, kicked up and down with both legs to launch his back, and smashed his left fist with a solid smack against the first man's cheek.

Again, he felt the warm, oily ooze of blood against his knuckles.

The first man's head whipped sideways. Long, curly hair danced about his shoulders. He mewled, sucked a raspy, enraged breath through his teeth that shone white in the darkness. Longarm hit him another, glancing blow. As the man sagged sideways off Longarm's hips, Longarm lurched to his feet, grabbed him by a handful of his curly hair, and held his head taut while he delivered three savage blows to the man's mouth and cheeks.

The man had been so stunned by the ferociousness of his opponent, that he hadn't even raised his hands to block the blows. He took them like a straw-filled dummy would take them, only this dummy grunted and sighed as his head jerked as though his neck swiveled on a spring.

Longarm released him, and he sagged to the ground, sort of sobbing and yowling at the same time, curling his legs into the fetal position and clapping his hands to his face.

The lawman turned to his second attacker, who'd been moving toward him, crouched and stealthy, fists raised. The man stopped suddenly. Longarm heard him swallow hard. The man dropped his hands, wheeled, and ran around the far side of the icehouse, his footsteps receding quickly in the quiet night.

Longarm turned to the man's friend, who was grunting and groaning as he climbed to one knee, cupping the underside of his lower right jaw as though to hold it in place. "I don't know who you are, you bastard!" He heaved himself to his feet. His eyes flashed sparks of fury, long hair dancing around his shoulders. "But you won't get far, you son of a bitch."

As he turned away, Longarm said, "Oh, I reckon we'll be chinnin' tomorrow, all right. When you're feelin' better. I'm at Dragoman Lodge."

The man turned back to him as though surprised by that bit of news. Then he staggered around the icehouse, dragging his boot toes, heading in the direction of the bunkhouse.

Longarm turned then, as well, and started back to the lodge.

# Chapter 12

Longarm woke before dawn the next morning and dressed by the light of a coal oil lamp.

He had no idea how early Dragoman rose, but since the man had said he was an early riser, he was likely up by now. Best to talk to the man about the icehouse stiff before anyone else was around. Murder—or the possibility of murder—was best discussed in private.

When Longarm had made his way downstairs, however, he realized that his discussion was not going to be a private one, after all. Several male voices, including that of Dragoman himself, emanated from the lodge's west end. Holding his snuff brown Stetson in his hand, Longarm followed the low rumbling through a large, carpeted parlor, then flipped the latch on a heavy, timbered door bedecked with a badger hide and stepped into the dining room.

He stopped just beyond the door and arched a curious brow.

The voices died, and the faces of the six men sitting at the long dining room table, including that of Dragoman, turned toward Longarm. Dragoman gave a delighted smile over the rim of the chipped, stone coffee mug he held in front of his chin.

He sat at the far end of the table, where he'd been sitting last night. On either side were five men dressed in rugged mountain gear, their hats piled to one side. One of the men, a flat-featured lad in his early twenties, had long, wavy brown hair tumbling to his shoulders. While the hair was thick and wild, it did not conceal the blood-spotted bandage over his ear. Nor the bruises and lacerations on his cheeks and jaws, a couple of them bristling stitches.

He sat on the opposite side of the table from Longarm, directly to Dragoman's left. The man who sat beside the long-haired gent glowered at Longarm around a nose that was swollen to twice its normal size and was the yellow-tinged purple of a stormy summer sky.

"Marshal!" Dragoman intoned, grinning delightedly. "Sleep well? You appear fit as a fiddle. Come on over here and meet my son and the men who work for me." His cunning eyes shifted to the two men sitting to his left. "But then, you've already met a couple of them, haven't you?"

Longarm moved forward, tossing his hat in his hands. "Indeed I have. In fact, I was sort of hopin' you and I could talk in private for a spell."

"Balderdash!" Dragoman exclaimed, setting his cup down and leaning back in his chair. "I let my men in on all the doin's about the lodge. Come, come." He gestured at the place setting at the far end of the table, a good stretch from himself and the other men, where he could keep an eye on his law-bringing visitor. "Have a seat. McCallum will be serving breakfast shortly."

Longarm heard a footstep behind him. He'd just started

to swing his head to the left when he saw the flap of his coat sweep back. A thick, red-brown hand closed over the butt of his .44-40 and slipped it up and out of its holster before Longarm could even begin to reach for it. Longarm turned his head back farther.

The big Indian, Wolf, flanked him, a faint smile lighting the native's chocolate brown eyes. He held Longarm's pistol down low in his right hand. He wore a big bowie on each stout hip, in addition to a holstered pistol in a beaded, tanned leather holster.

Longarm turned back to Dragoman, still grinning at him with mild amusement, a faint, delighted deviousness glinting in his pale blue eyes. The lawman returned the look. "Things are growing right interesting around here."

"There's never a dull moment at Dragoman Lodge." Dragoman nodded at an empty chair on the table's right side. "Do sit down, Marshal."

"You got enough guns, Dragoman. Why take mine?"

"Speaking of guns," Dragoman said, looking at Wolf still flanking Longarm, "check him for more."

Wolf jammed the lawman's own pistol into his ribs— so hard it hurt—and thumbed the hammer back. Holding the gun there, he patted Longarm down, coming up with the gold-plated, pearl-gripped, over-and-under derringer in Longarm's right vest pocket. The watch came out of the other pocket, dangling by its gold-washed chain.

Wolf held up the gun and the watch for Dragoman to see.

"Is that all you're carrying, Marshal Long?"

"I reckon it is."

Longarm tried to suppress the burn of rage that welled up from his spine and spread as it climbed his back. He didn't like being relieved of his weapons. What's more, he didn't like walking into a trap whistling as innocently as some towheaded schoolboy hauling a bouquet of wild-flowers back home to his mom.

"I probably don't need to tell you that relieving a federal lawman of the weapons of his trade is a right nasty thing to do, not to mention a federal offense."

"I hope you don't think that's going to change my mind." The good humor leached from the lodge master's eyes. "Sit. Have some breakfast. You're going to need it."

Wolf jammed Longarm's pistol against his spine—again hard enough to cause Longarm to raise a cheek in silent protest. He looked at the place setting at the near end of the table, several places down from the two nearest men—far enough away that he couldn't do any damage with, say, a table knife or a fork if he had a mind to physically protest his having been relieved of his weapons. And maybe throw a punch or two before these men—all big enough and likely capable—subdued him.

Longarm dragged the chair out and sank into it. He slid forward and crossed his arms at the table's edge, staring coldly straight down the ten-foot length of the oilcloth-covered table at the master of Dragoman Lodge.

"I reckon the obvious question," he said, "is why am I going to need it? I was sorta thinking about having a nap later. I hate napping on a full belly."

"Oh, you won't be napping."

Dragoman turned to his right as the cook, McCallum, walked into the room with two large, steaming platters—one with scrambled eggs, the other covered with fried potatoes. Wolf's sister, the round-faced, black-haired Sumah, shuffled in behind him carrying two more platters—one heaped with side pork, the other with flapjacks.

"It's about time, McCallum," Dragoman said gruffly. "We got us a hunt on this morning."

"Sorry, sir," the beefy, gray-haired Scot said as he set his two platters on the table, then turned to take Suma's platters and set them down, as well.

"Will you be joining us?"

McCallum straightened. He was a red-faced man who wore his long gray hair in a ragged ponytail. He wore buckskins and an apron. As he studied Longarm, a strange expression entered the man's green-eyed gaze, one so cold and feral that it took Longarm aback for a moment. And, for another moment, he thought he had a handle on what was happening, though after that second stretched moment had passed, he mentally shrugged it off.

No. That couldn't be it.

It was far more pedestrian that that. One of these men had simply though criminally murdered another, and his boss and son and the others were merely trying to protect him, though they'd gone about it all the wrong way. They'd gone too far. And now, of course, there was no going back. No going anywhere but in front of a judge.

Longarm felt deep regret that Cynthia was involved, and that this man was part of her family, but he hadn't called the dance.

Dragoman had. And he'd be punished for it.

So much for Longarm's vacation. But he'd had a feeling it was over last night after he'd found the stiff in the icehouse and the fisticuffs that followed.

The Scot shuttled his wild, bright-eyed gaze to his boss, eagerly wiping his brown, greasy hands on his apron. "I do believe I'll join you, Mr. Dragoman, sir. Sumah'll see the ladies when they rise."

Stone-faced, Sumah turned around and headed back to the kitchen.

"Very good," Dragoman said. "The more the merrier. You'll want to eat, then, as well, before we go. Which will be soon."

McCallum nodded and strode back to the kitchen behind Sumah.

As he forked a chunk of side pork onto his plate, Dragoman glanced at Wolf. "Have the horses brought up. For the marshal, bring up that skewbald paint. The stallion. He won't be needing it after we get to the knob, but I know the marshal is a man who appreciates fine horseflesh."

The scrambled eggs had made it to the man on Longarm's right, and as Wolf left the room in his lumbering stride, the man looked at Longarm with that same hungry, white-ringed look in his eyes as he set the bowl of eggs down on the table and slid it toward Longarm.

"You're about to have the tables turned, Marshal," Dragoman said, helping himself to two big flapjacks. "You've hunted men. I don't doubt you've hunted them down and killed them. Well, now you'll have men hunting you."

Longarm stared down the length of the table at the man again. His pulse itched in his wrists, and his blood rushed in his ears. Dragoman didn't look crazy—or he hadn't looked crazy until this morning. But now, his eyes looked flatter, the pupils larger and darker. The whites looked whiter. He had the same eager, anticipatory look that McCallum had had, and that all the rest of these men still wore. Dragoman's son was grinning through the bruises on his swollen face as he forked a ragged chunk of side pork into his mouth.

"Goddamnit, Bentley!" the master of Dragoman lodge yelled suddenly and slammed the back of his hand against his son's broad mouth. "What did I tell you about eating before everyone else's plate is filled? How dare you embarrass me like this?" He canted his head to get a better view of the young man's bloody ear. "Embarrass yourself in front of the men. You, too, Parnell," he added to the man with the balloon-sized nose.

Parnell glowered. At least, he appeared to glower. It was hard to tell if he was flushed or simply swollen. He glanced at Longarm, then dropped his eyes to his plate and gritted his teeth until his jaws quivered.

"Letting yourselves get taken down like this. Both of you." Dragoman shook his head and laughed and laughed caustically. "By one man."

"He's a big son of a bitch, Pa. And faster than he looks like he'd be."

"A formidable foe, eh?" Dragoman studied Longarm anew, that predatory look of delight in his eyes again. Finally, he indicated the food platters that had piled up in front of the lawman. "Please, Marshal. We can't eat until you've filled your plate. English manners, you know. Then we'll go out and make a day of it."

Longarm drew a deep breath. He'd found himself in many an unfortunate situation. But this was one to start his memoirs with . . . if he lived to recount them. He looked at the food. Fear hadn't diminished his appetite in many a day. In fact, it stoked it. He had a feeling that Dragoman was right—this was a day to begin with a full belly.

So he began filling his plate, first with the eggs and flapjacks and then side pork and potatoes. He filled his coffee cup from the big, black pot sitting on a trivet in the middle of the table, then went to work shoveling the food into his mouth, asking, "You got tired of hunting animals, I take it? Wild animals, I mean? That dead fella in the icehouse your new brand of prey, Dragoman?"

The other men looked at Dragoman. Chewing slowly, he appeared considering how much he was going to disclose. He hiked a shoulder, probed the gap between his front teeth with his tongue, then reached for his coffee mug. "No, he was one of my men. The damn fool let his quarry get the drop on him. A Chinaman from the village. We found him out cutting wood. A loner. Since likely no one would miss him—except those he was cutting wood for, I reckon—we hauled him up here." Dragoman sipped from the mug. "The Chinaman was slightly more game than my man, Lutz, had anticipated. Our quarry sharpened a stick, lay in wait, and, according to my son, gutted Lutz till he bled out like a pig."

"Don't worry—he paid for it, Pa," Bentley said, showing a mouthful of egg through a grin. "Took him down with that Sharps you gave me for my birthday."

"I hope with one shot."

"Of course!"

Longarm slowed his own chewing down. So, he'd been right. A worm turned in the bottom of his belly, beneath the food he was putting down. He remembered Alma and Angus Thompson. Had their father been one of Dragoman's quarries? The thought nearly killed his hunger, but he knew he was going to need all the sustenance he could pack down, so he kept eating.

He tried not to worry about Cynthia. She'd be all right, he told himself. She was Dragoman's niece, after all. Certainly this man, crazed by too many years alone, season after season, year after year, in these remote mountains, had not lured his niece up here to hunt her.

No. Couldn't be. The man wanted "formidable foes," and Cynthia would be far from that. Longarm, however, offered an irresistible sporting challenge. And since the lawman had already stumbled onto clues to Dragoman's secret game, and started asking questions that could go nowhere but to the heart of these dastardly doings, he'd suddenly become fair game himself.

He couldn't quite believe this was happening. It felt like a four-year-old's fever dream. But he'd better start believing it, he told himself. Because, judging by the savage, hungry looks on the men eating around him now and cunningly taking his measure, he was going to be hunted like any stock-murdering wolf.

*Thanks for the vacation, Billy.*

# Chapter 13

Longarm felt the hammering blow of cold water engulfing his face and head. His ears rang. An impenetrable chill pressed against him.

He swam up out of the murky darkness of unconsciousness and instinctively fought to lift his head from the water, but something was holding him down.

Several hands, most likely. He felt the knuckles of one biting into the back of his neck.

His lungs felt pinched down to the size of raisins, and his chest felt as though a railroad spike had been driven through it. Finally, the brusque hands on his collar jerked his head up. The cold water streamed down his face and, hearing his own raspy rake of badly needed air, he blinked and looked straight out in front of him.

He was on the rocky bank of a fast-moving stream tumbling down the floor of a steep, narrow canyon. He was on his hands and knees, and the back of his head throbbed. The ache brought back the dull memory of walking out

the back door of Dragoman Lodge and suddenly feeling
something hard—a pistol butt, most likely—driven through
the crown of his hat.

Everything was dark after that, though he'd been vaguely
aware of riding a saddled horse with his hands tied to the
saddle horn, his ankles bound to stirrups. His sleep had
been multilayered, and in the shallowest layers he'd heard
voices and had entertained the yearning for the trip to be
over.

His head felt as though it had been split open to expose
his tender brain, and the rocking of the horse over rugged
terrain hadn't done anything to diminish the little man
perched atop inside and rapping away at him every five
seconds with a hammer and chisel.

"Where the fuck are we?" he growled, spitting water
from his lips, hacking it up from his lungs.

"This is Goat Head Creek," said Dragoman's deep voice
behind him, above the stream's rush as it tumbled and
sprayed over rocks. "You're a mile from the lodge."

Longarm jerked around, water leaping off of him.
Dragoman's son and the man with the broken nose, Parnell, leaped back as though afraid of getting wet. Dragoman stood a few yards away, casually smoking a briar
pipe. The other four men, including Wolf and the cook,
McCallum, flanked him in a line. Behind them were saddled horses, one for each man including Longarm, absently pulling at the knee-high bluestem growing along
the streambed.

"Why the hell the clubbing, you fuckin' coward?"

"Hey," said Parnell. "Don't talk to the boss like that."

"Who was the coward who rapped me on the head?
Something tells me it was you, little man. The one who
ran from the fight last night, tail between his legs."

Dragoman's son snickered.

Parnell lowered his head and ran toward Longarm. The lawman stepped sideways, grabbed the collar of the man's rat-hair coat, and slammed his head into a tree bole.

*"Whoah!"* Parnell said.

Longarm rammed his right fist into the man's ear. The man's head jerked sideways. Longarm rammed his fist into the man's head again, and then, grabbing him by his coat and the waistband of his duck trousers, spun him around and into the stream, where he hit with a splash and lay facedown, flopping his arms and trying feebly to lift his head from the water.

"Damn, this is gonna be a hunt to remember, boys!" Dragoman intoned, holding his pipe up near his lips, slapping a thigh, and howling.

The other men smiled, equally delighted.

Dragoman looked at his son, then nodded toward where Parnell was beginning to slide off downstream. Bentley trudged into the water, grabbed Parnell's collar just before the little hard case had started to be pulled off around a waterlogged tree, and dragged him to shore. Bentley left Parnell in the rocks, where the broken-nosed man rose onto his hands and knees, coughing wildly and shaking his head.

Bentley glowered at Longarm. "Yeah, this'll be fun, Pa."

Dragoman walked over to a tall, cream barb. He removed from his saddle horn a bowie knife and scabbard. He tossed the knife at Longarm's boots. "That'll be your only weapon. Don't worry, it's sharp."

Dragoman grinned. Then he removed a small pouch from his saddlebags, and tossed it, too, onto the ground at Longarm's feet.

"There's four strips of deer jerky in there. That oughta get you started. I'm sure you'll figure out some other way to get food . . . if you live long enough to get hungry again."

Longarm looked at the knife. "That's the only weapon I get?"

"That's all I'm givin' you. You can, of course, use whatever else you find."

"A little unfair, ain't it? I assume you'll be using guns."

"That we will—one rifle and one pistol each and only three bullets apiece in each weapon."

Longarm laughed.

"And we'll be coming one man at a time," Dragoman said. "The first man will come one hour from now. The rest of us will follow every half hour after that."

"How do you decide the order?"

"We draw straws," Bentley said. He was puffing a stogie, the smoke rising around his head and the white, blood-spotted bandage on his right ear. He was fingering the stitches high on his right cheek.

Longarm narrowed an eye at the obvious insane master of Dragoman lodge. "What about your niece? What about Cynthia?"

"She'll be fine," Dragoman said, frowning. "I didn't bring either of you out here to be hunted. You walked into this game yourself, Marshal. Since my son was stupid enough to deposit Lutz where he could be found"—he cast a reprimanding look at Bentley—"and you found him, you were bound to find out more."

"Not necessarily."

"Well," Dragoman said with a shrug, shoving his pipe into the breast pocket of his long, bearskin greatcoat, "there was a chance. I just couldn't take it. Or overlook the amazing opportunity you provided. Hunting a hunter. And a human one, at that. Couldn't pass that up now, could I?"

Longarm picked up the knife in the tanned leather sheath. The other men were grabbing their reins and mounting their horses. Parnell was rising, breathing hard and holding a hand to his right ear, which was cut and swollen up to match the battered one of Bentley's.

"What if I head to town?" Longarm said. Gothic was likely the only one within a half a day's horse ride. He didn't know how far from where he was, however.

Dragoman had grabbed his saddle horn and was pulling himself into the leather with a grunt. When he'd gotten settled, he hiked a shoulder. "I wouldn't head that way, myself. Too many deep canyons between here and there. You'll likely get trapped in one. But that's entirely up to you."

"And if I get there?"

Dragoman directed a serious gaze at Longarm, the corners of his eyes stretching short lines. "Then you're free. None of us will touch you once you've made it to Gothic. But no one we've hunted has made it there yet. You'll obviously prove to be the most challenging prey my men and I have ever hunted—it's mainly been aimless drifters and old prospectors, a few Chinese rail workers up to now—but we're pretty crafty ourselves. I doubt you'll make it. But, like I said, if you do make it, you'll be free."

Longarm wanted to ask him if he knew that that would mean not only the end to his crazy, savage game but also the end of Dragoman himself. He saw no point in bringing that up, however. His main concern for the time being was to stay alive and to get Cynthia away from Dragoman Lodge as soon as he could. Dragoman might sincerely love his niece, but no one was safe at the lodge.

Longarm wondered vaguely if Dragoman's daughter, Lucy, had gone as loco as her father and brother had. She hadn't seemed crazy, but then, neither had Dragoman when Longarm had first met the man.

"What're you going to tell Cynthia?"

Dragoman shrugged. "That we went out riding, and you got separated from me and my men. We looked everywhere, but this is vast country out here."

Dragoman looked smugly satisfied.

"There's plenty of water around," he said, changing the subject. "Food, too, if you know how to hunt it with a knife. I'm sure you'll come to see this as a rousing challenge yourself. Good luck, Marshal."

The man actually seemed to mean it, Longarm thought as Dragoman neck-reined his horse around and booted it downstream. The other men, including Parnell, who glanced malevolently over his shoulder at Longarm, followed the man along the trees lining the stream. They followed a bend out of sight, the thuds of their horses' hooves dwindling gradually behind them.

Then there was only the stream's rush over rocks. The twitter of birds. The breeze rustling the late summer leaves.

And the steady, heavy thuds of Longarm's heart.

An hour later, he dug his fingers into a crack in the rock wall he was climbing, pressed the toes of his cavalry boots onto a slight shelf, and pulled and pushed himself up, gritting his teeth with the effort.

He'd left the stream, as there'd been only open ground out there, and had moved southeast along the canyon the stream had cut. He hadn't bothered covering his tracks, for he didn't hope to outrun the hunting party. What he hoped to do was to turn the tables on each of them, turn each into the quarry. Kill them one by one.

All he needed was to capture one pistol and/or a rifle and some shells, as well as a horse, and he'd have a good start on fulfilling his plan.

The crest of the rock wall inched lower, so that he could see the roots angling down over the lip. There was a forest up there with a shallow dirt floor sending up bits of needlegrass. There'd been easier routes up the slope and into the trees, but the rock wall would leave little trace of his passing. A man riding below the ridge would think he'd continued on along the narrow, gravelly trail threading this side canyon, and should be easy prey to the bowie, if he could throw the damn thing straight. He'd once been good with a knife, but he was out of practice. Lawdogging didn't include much knife work.

One misstep here would be deadly.

He reached for the lip of the ridge. A hand and wrist appeared out of nowhere. Longarm's lower jaw had started to drop in awe when he saw the light brown hand at the end of an arm clad in red-and-black wool plaid close around his wrist.

There was a low grunt. The arm pulled, lifting Longarm's hand up from the ridgetop, and suddenly Longarm's entire body was jerked straight up the canyon wall. His belly ground painfully against the wall's sharp lip edge, and then he was belly down on the forest floor, only his ankles and feet dangling over the wall, and staring at two high-topped, lace-up boots into which corduroy trousers had been tucked.

The boots were old and scuffed. Dried blood was crusted on both toes.

Longarm lifted his gaze up the man's legs and past his two belt buckles to his chest clad in an age-worn sheepskin vest and then to the nut-colored face capped with a thick mop of long, silver hair dropping down from a leather-billed, black felt cap. The cook, McCallum, grinned down at Longarm, wet brown lips pooched out as he worked the chew in his mouth. In his right hand, the cook held a knife much like the one that Dragoman had given Longarm.

McCallum had a turquoise-studded silver ring on his little finger. It bulged as the man squeezed the hide-wrapped handle of the knife harder with malicious zeal.

"A little early, aren't you?" Longarm growled.

McCallum gave another grunt, then leaned down, grabbed the back of Longarm's coat, and pulled the lawman up onto his feet. He continued pulling him past his own body as he pivoted on his hips, and slammed him headfirst into the trunk of a tall fir. Longarm had managed to cushion the blow with his right forearm. Still, bells tolled in his ears, his neck felt as though a railroad spike had been hammered through it from the back, and his compacted spine throbbed.

He dropped to his knees.

Longarm shook his head to clear the cobwebs, then heaved himself, breathless and aching his body over, to his feet. He turned. McCallum stood three feet away, a savage grin on the man's broad, weathered face and in his flashing blue eyes.

"This ain't gonna be near as hard as ole Dragoman thought, is it, me laddie? And with only me pigsticker, no less!"

McCallum's right fist, squeezing the hide-wrapped haft, slammed toward Longarm in a bright, wicked flash of yellow sunlight off the razor-edged steel. Longarm ducked and sidestepped. The blade of the knife thudded into the fir, broken bark dropping away from the tip.

Longarm pivoted left, burying his right fist into the cook's belly. The man doubled over, lines of agony digging across his forehead, but somehow managed to keep his hand on the knife, which, with one hard pull, he removed from the fir trunk. He staggered back, his face flushed, his breath and bulging belly rising and falling heavily.

With a single, loud intake of air, he recovered and squared his shoulders and hips, jostling the knife in his right hand, turning it this way and that in his now loosely clenched fist. His wicked grin stretched across his broad mouth once more.

Longarm slipped his own knife from the sheath he'd attached to his belt and squared his own hips and shoulders. The cook's smile broadened. The men squared off, side-stepping. When they'd traced nearly a complete circle, the cook lunged forward, poking his bowie toward Longarm's belly. It was a halfhearted, probing lunge, testing the lawman's reflexes.

When the cook lunged again, harder and faster, Longarm smashed the blade of his own knife against that of the cook's, the wicked screech of clashing steel shattering the near silence of the forest. Again, they squared off, Longarm shuttling his anxiety-bright gaze between the knife in the cook's fist and the man's crazed eyes.

Longarm lunged, his knife tip kissing the man's wool shirt, then pulled back. The cook swept his own knife crossways as though to parry the blow. When the momentum of his own thrust had carried his knife out beyond his left arm, Longarm swiped his own bowie at an angle across the man's right upper arm.

The cook winced. Stepping back, he glanced at the blood
oozing from the quarter-inch-deep gash. He looked at
Longarm, and his features hardened for a moment before
he formed an expression of pathological rage.

He lunged forward, and Longarm had to work like hell
to parry the savage slashes directed at his belly, chest, and
throat. When he'd been driven back almost to the edge
of the cliff, he saw a brief opening, and lunged forward.
The cook's rage had turned him into a knife-fighting machine, and McCallum slammed the blade of his own bowie
across Longarm's blade so hard that the knife flew out of
the lawdog's hand.

It arced high, then hit the spongy forest floor with a
tinny rasp.

McCallum opened his mouth saucer-wide and loosed
an ear-rattling roar. He lunged off his heels, bulling toward Longarm with his knife held carelessly high and out
away from his body. As his body bolted toward Longarm, and the knife careened toward the lawman's head,
Longarm reached up, grabbed the plunging wrist in both
his own big hands, pivoted, putting his back to the cook,
and flipped McCallum over his right shoulder.

McCallum hit the ground on his back, rolled backward, and disappeared over the side of the ridge.

Below, a horse whinnied. A girl gave a clipped scream.
Hooves thudded wildly, clacking on the stony trail as though
trying to regain its footing, and then a man's agonized
groan rose.

Longarm lurched forward to peer over the lip of the
ridge. His eyes snapped wide in disbelief.

As a fine-boned chestnut galloped off up the trail, stirrups flapping like wings, McCallum sprawled belly down
on the canyon floor. Nearby, in rustic riding slacks, white

blouse, and leather vest, a girl was pushing herself up onto her hands and knees after apparently being unseated from her horse by McCallum's plunging bulk.

Cynthia tossed her long, straight, jet black hair back over her shoulder and looked up at Longarm in wild befuddlement.

# Chapter 14

*"Cynthia!"*

Longarm scrambled down the wall so quickly that his boot slipped out of a crack and he dropped the last ten feet to the trail, landing on his heels and plunging straight backward. He hit the trail so hard on his back that stars danced in his eyes and bells tolled in his ears.

He pushed himself up, grumbling, and half walked, half crawled over to where Cynthia now lay on her back, propped on her elbows, one leg curled beneath her. Her hair obscured her pale cheeks, and she continued to blink her eyes, her crisp white, high-button blouse riding and falling heavily as she breathed.

"Cynthia." Longarm dropped his head down close to hers and slid her hair back away from her face. "Tell me you're all right, girl." He glanced at McCallum, who lay unconscious on the other side of the trail, on his back, his arms and legs akimbo. Blood trickled from a corner of his mouth. Longarm hardened his jaws in fury. Of course, he'd thrown McCallum off the ledge, but Cynthia wouldn't be lying on the trail right now if the man hadn't come after Longarm in this crazy game of Dragoman's.

Cynthia shook her head and opened her eyes wide, turning her head slowly toward Longarm. "Custis . . . ?"

Longarm continued to slide her cheeks back away from her face. "You all right?" He ran his hands down her sides, gently probing. "You all right, girl? Anything broke, you think?"

Cynthia slid her right leg out from under her left thigh, wincing a little. "No. I think I'm just bruised. Oh, Custis, I'm so sorry I got you into this." She sobbed and, sitting up, grabbed his right arm, pulled him toward her, and wrapped both her own arms around his neck. "I'm so sorry!"

Longarm held her, squeezing her gently, still afraid she might have broken a rib or two in her tumble from the Dragoman horse. "What're you doin' out here?"

"I saw." She convulsed in a sob as she pressed her heaving bosom tight against his chest. "I saw them carry you away from the lodge. Saw them throw you onto that horse and ride away." She pulled slightly away from him and sandwiched his cheeks in her hands, tears dribbling down her own cheeks now to which some color was finally returning. "I went down to the barn and saddled a horse. No one was around to stop me."

"You followed us out here?"

Cynthia nodded. "Well, I tried. You were too far ahead of me, but I nearly ran into Uncle Charles and his men a half hour ago. He didn't see me. I rode around them and . . ." She shook her head in total disbelief of the situation. "And here I am." Slowly, she turned her face toward McCallum, who lay unmoving in the middle of the trail, one boot propped on a rock.

"You shouldn't have come out here, girl."

"What was I supposed to do when I saw my uncle and cousin and all his men haul you away from the lodge like so much dirty laundry? I had no idea what was going on." She blinked her wide blue eyes. "And I still don't." She clutched at him desperately. "Custis, what on earth is *happening*?"

She winced suddenly and, releasing him, reached for her own left shoulder. *"Ohh!"*

"What is it?"

"Damn—it's my shoulder. It hurts like a son of a bitch!"

"Such talk comin' from the general's favorite niece," Longarm muttered, using dry humor to undercut his own fear for the girl's safety.

He took her left forearm in his right hand, moved it gently upward. Cynthia sucked a sharp breath through gritted teeth. Longarm stayed the movement, and looked around, his heavy brows furled, his leathery cheeks flushed with alarm. "Probably sprained. We gotta get you off the trail. One more will be coming soon . . . and then one more every half hour after that."

"Custis," Cynthia urged, holding her left shoulder and staring up at him in disbelief. "Please tell me what is going on here. What is Uncle Charles *doing*?"

Longarm returned her gaze. There was no point in hiding the truth from her. Not now that she was out here and in much the same boat as Longarm himself. "I don't know quite how to tell you this, Cynthia. But your uncle is a cold-blooded killer. I don't know what he was like before, but he's obviously crazier'n a treeful of owls now."

She just stared at him, cobalt blue eyes narrowed in utter perplexity and beseeching.

"Him and his boys are hunting me."

She continued to gaze at him for a moment, her addled brain slow to comprehend what he'd just told her. It was a raspy whisper: *"What!"*

Longarm heaved himself to his feet, walked over to where McCallum lay unmoving, and dropped to a knee beside the man. He pressed two fingers to the cook's neck. No pulse. The trail beneath his head was blood soaked. Apparently, a cracked skull. Likely a broken back and neck, as well. It was a good hundred-foot fall. He must have only grazed Cynthia when he'd dislodged her from her horse, or she'd be in a lot worse shape than she was.

Again, fury burned through Longarm. He looked at Cynthia. She might very easily be dead. He peered past her to the trail beyond. Another hunter would be coming soon. He had to get her out of here, get her hid where none of Dragoman's men could find her. No telling what they might do if they knew she was out here.

Out here with the lawman they were hunting like a rabid coyote.

Obviously, they were all as crazy as Dragoman himself.

Longarm dragged McCallum about twenty yards off the trail, into a snag of willows and chokecherries where he'd likely be found, as Longarm didn't have time to conceal the body properly. His main concern at the moment was getting Cynthia somewhere safe. He took the man's cartridge belt, and holstered pistol, which, as Dragoman had promised, contained only three shells. Buckling the belt and gun around his waist, Longarm returned to the trail.

"Come on, girl," he said, taking Cynthia's arm and

gently pulling her up. "Gotta get you out of here. Gotta get you hid somewhere."

"No." She winced again at a stab of pain in her shoulder and pulled away from Longarm. "I'm going to stay right here. Uncle Charles will be along soon, won't he?"

Longarm's frown deepened. "That's the problem, sweetheart."

"You can't think that . . . ?" She let her voice trail off, and the skin above the bridge of her nose wrinkled. "That he'd do any harm to me . . . his own . . ." Again she let her voice trail off.

"I'll tell you one thing," Longarm said pointedly. "I ain't gonna let you stand out here to find out." He looked down trail, in the direction in which Cynthia's horse had galloped off. "I wonder if I could run him down."

"Her," Cynthia said. "It's a mare. And she's skittish as hell. I'd say she's long gone, Custis."

Longarm lifted his gaze up the ridge, scouring the towering pines. "McCallum must have his horse up there somewhere."

"He's dead, eh?" Cynthia looked into the brush where Longarm had dragged the cook, a sort of wistful look of regret on her features. Before Longarm could say anything, she said, "He . . . tried to kill you?"

It would take her a while to work her mind around all of this, but Longarm didn't have time to let her do it here. He had to get her someplace relatively safe and then scout the ridge he'd just left for McCallum's horse.

He took Cynthia's arm. "Can you walk or should I carry you?"

"It's only my shoulder that's injured. I can walk." She put some steel into her voice now and looked up at him reassuringly though the fear and confusion were still there, as well.

Longarm adjusted McCallum's pistol on his right hip, then took Cynthia's hand and led her off the trail and into the scrub brush beyond. The canyon was broader than it had looked before.

They'd walked about twenty minutes, over a low hill carpeted in wheatgrass, when they came to the lip of a wash strewn with brush and boulders. There were two forks of a creek though only the near fork had any water in it—a thin, muddy trickle running between the rocks. Up the wash a ways was another sheer ridge, but at the base of the ridge appeared to be several shallow notch caves.

Good hiding places.

When he had Cynthia tucked away in one such cave, which was well concealed by boulders and a gnarled willow, he removed his string tie and wrapped it around Cynthia's own neck. She looked up at him. "He's gone mad, then, hasn't he?"

She had a slight scrape above her right brow and on the nub of her right cheek. Her eyes were clearer now, keener. The knowledge was sinking in.

"Like I said—crazier'n a treefull of owls."

"And he's hunting you?"

"That's right. Him and your cousin, Bentley, and Wolf and about three other hired men from the bunkhouse." Longarm looked around as he gathered the loose ends of his thoughts. Turning back to Cynthia, he said, "Where's Cousin Lucy?"

"She was still in her room when I left the lodge."

"So she didn't come with you."

"No."

"Good."

Cynthia winced as Longarm gently eased her right forearm through the makeshift sling he'd fashioned for her. "You don't think Lucy's part of this crazy charade, do you?"

"Sure as hell seems like everyone else is." Longarm placed his hands on Cynthia's shoulders and looked seriously into her eyes. "If you see her, don't call out—okay? Just in case."

Cynthia nodded as she lifted her good hand to reassuringly caress Longarm's forearm. "All right."

Longarm kissed her. "Sit tight. I'll be back soon."

He turned and, fingering the bone grips of McCallum's Colt .44, walked down the narrow wash and back to the main trail. At the place where McCallum had fallen on Cynthia, Longarm stopped and peered into the western distance, where the canyon opened wider and showed blue mountains under a clear, cerulean sky. There were several rocky upthrusts out there, between him and the higher ridges. He stared for several minutes, spying no coming riders.

He turned toward the ridge, not relishing the idea of climbing it again. Farther up trail it had looked a little lower. Deciding to head that way and maybe find where McCallum had climbed it—either on horseback or foot—he stopped in his tracks.

A rider, silhouetted against the vast sky and the mountains behind him, was coming at a spanking trot between low, sand-colored escarpments. Longarm dropped down behind a boulder at the base of the ridge to his left and peered out around the side of it. Hard to tell who the next hunter was. From this distance, it could have been any of the remaining five men. Even Dragoman.

Longarm looked around, again fingering the pistol in his holster.

About fifty yards down trail, there was a depression in the ground behind several scraggly pines. Retreating a dozen yards, until he was out of sight of the rider moving toward him, he scrambled off the trail's right side, and jogged into the gulch. Just behind the pines that formed a sort of door to the mouth of the canyon that Longarm was in, he hunkered down behind some rocks thrust up when the spring snowmelt had flooded the gulch and drew the bone-gripped .44.

He looked at the gun, spun the cylinder.

Three loads.

He'd have to make them count.

He crouched lower, drove his right shoulder up snug against the rocks. Hoof thuds sounded, growing quickly louder as the second hunter approached.

# Chapter 15

Longarm willed the stiffness from his limbs as the horse appeared on the trail to his left, clomping as it trotted up the narrow canyon that angled deep into a jog of high ridges. The lawman stood up, cocked the Colt as he extended it straight out from his shoulder, and said, "Hold it."

He hadn't gotten the second word out before he saw the horse's empty saddle. A half second later he heard boots crunch gravel behind him, and the low titter of delighted snickers. He wheeled as a gun barked, causing the horse now behind him to whinny.

Longarm hit the ground, rolling onto his belly and extending the Colt once more at the figure before him, one of the two men he hadn't met but whose name he'd heard was Stiles or some such—a stocky man with a hawk nose and deep-set eyes, with a thick mustache and three or four days of beard stubble on his pale cheeks. The man's dark eyes sparked with mocking laughter at the trick he'd just pulled, but as he swung his smoking rifle toward Longarm once more and triggered two more quick shots, both of which sailed wide of Longarm to spang off the rocks behind the lawman, his face pinched furiously.

He triggered another shot but the hammer dropped to the firing pin with a benign ping.

Longarm stayed his trigger finger, and curled his upper lip as he glared at the man through the man's own wafting gun smoke. "Hold it."

"Shit!" the man wheezed, looking at the smoking rifle in his hand as though it had suddenly turned into a coiled rattlesnake. He took it in his left hand and let it dangle down by his leg. His hand opened near the pistol thonged on his other thigh.

"Pull that hogleg, and you're a dead man," Longarm warned.

"You move fast for a big man—you know that?" the man said, his stubbled cheeks mottled red with exasperation. "Shit, I had you dead to rights."

Longarm heaved himself to his feet. "I take it you ain't the best shot of Dragoman's crazy bunch."

Frustration bit him. What was he going to do with this man? By rights, he should kill him. That would save him a lot of trouble. But he just couldn't do it. Not now that the man wasn't bearing down on him. He knew that this nod to the law and what was just plain right was liable to get him killed, and endanger Cynthia's life even further, but he couldn't just pop a pill through the man's forehead to get him out of his way.

Dragoman would do that to Longarm. He had that on his side. But Longarm couldn't do it.

"Nice and slow, lift that pistol from its holster and toss it over here near me. You so much as flinch, you're a dead man."

The man's long coat hung open, brushing the tops of his boots, as he slowly lifted his right hand to the hogleg, lifted the piece from its holster, and with a chuff of deep frustration, tossed it onto the gravel a couple of feet from Longarm's cavalry boots.

Longarm glanced at the trail. He felt a little grin of relief lift his mouth corners when he saw that the man's horse, a dapple gray, was standing only a few yards farther up the trail than where Longarm had last seen him.

The lawman strode forward, holding his cocked Colt a foot out from his belly, aimed at the stocky, hawk-faced gent before him. Now that he was closer, he thought he'd seen that face before. A Wanted dodger? He wouldn't doubt it. "What do you do for Dragoman?" he asked him.

"I tend his horses. What's it to you?"

"How long you been workin' for him?"

The man frowned uncertainly and narrowed a dark eye. "Two years."

"How long has he been hunting men?"

The man grinned suddenly, mockingly. "I ain't tellin' you a damn thing, lawdog."

"All right."

"No, wait!" The man lifted his arms but not before Longarm had slammed the butt of his pistol against the side of the man's head.

He piled up like a sack of parched corn at the lawman's feet.

"My God," Cynthia said. "Who's that?"

"One of the hunters." Longarm pulled the dapple gray up into the nest of rocks fronting the notch cave and glanced at the man whom he'd slung over the dapple's back, behind the saddle. "Name's Morgan Stiles. Found it on a scrap of paper when I was scrounging in his saddle-bags for rope to tie him. Market hunter from Nebraska. Wanted for murder and rape, if I remember correctly." The lawman swung down from the saddle. "He's harmless as a pet turtle now, though."

"My god—a murderer and rapist . . . working for Uncle Charles."

"I don't think you oughta regard him as your old uncle Charles, sweetheart," Longarm said as he slid the unconscious killer down the dapple's hindquarters. "The man who's after us, or at least after me, bears little inner resemblance to the man you remember."

Cynthia stood beside a boulder, her arm in a sling. Her hair and the brown leather vest she wore over her blouse jostled in the cooling afternoon breeze. She stared as Longarm dragged the man by his ankles into the rocks near the cave. "I don't understand this. Any of it. It's all so bizarre, Custis. Crazy."

"It is at that."

Longarm had gagged Stiles with the man's own neckerchief. Now he rolled the man as far back into the notch cave as he could, so he couldn't be seen from the trail above the ravine. As he straightened, the rattle of a bridle chain and bit sounded in the near distance.

Cynthia, whose own hearing wasn't as keen as the lawman's, had just opened her mouth to speak. Longarm quickly pressed a finger to his lips, shushing her, and stared westward along the ridge running along the ravine.

"What is it?" Cynthia whispered.

"Another visitor." Longarm hurried forward and, closing his hand over the dapple's snout with one hand, to keep it from sounding the alarm, and tugging its reins with the other, led the horse as far back into the rocks fronting the cave as he could. He beckoned Cynthia, and she came up to stand beside him, facing the ridge.

"I led them here, didn't I?" she whispered.

"McCallum cut my own sign before he had time to cut yours."

Longarm extended the dapple's reins to Cynthia. She took them, frowning at him curiously.

"I'm going to see what's happening up there." Longarm adjusted Stiles's revolver on his right hip. He had McCallum's .44 wedged behind the waistband of his slacks. Six shots. He canted his head at the horse. "Can you keep him quiet?"

"Sure." Cynthia stepped up close to the dapple and held the same hand in which she held the reins over the horse's nostrils in case it tried to whinny.

Longarm drew the Colt he'd taken off McCallum and walked slowly down the wash. He kept his eye on the ridgeline above his head. He could hear the horseback rider moving toward him, and when the man was about twenty feet beyond him, Longarm stopped and pressed his back against the wash's rocky wall, holding the cocked Colt barrel up near his shoulder.

The hoof thuds stopped. Apparently, the rider was checking out the sign on the trail. Longarm had wiped out as much of it as he could with a downed branch to which several pine needles still clung, but if Dragoman's men were the trackers he suspected they were, they'd read what he'd done. Or what he'd tried to do.

Longarm kept his back pressed against the wash's wall, squeezing the gun in his hands. When the man came down here, following the sign that Longarm had likely left in the brittle grass, he'd try to use one shot. A clean shot through the head, to conserve ammunition.

He was surprised when the hoof thuds sounded again and the horse and rider passed behind him along the trail above his head, back in the direction of the higher ridges that jutted from deeper down canyon. Of course, there was always a chance the man was pulling the same trick that Stiles had. But when Longarm had pulled himself up the wall and stood in the trail, he saw the horse and rider dwindling into the northeastern distance, still not too far away for Longarm to recognize the long, blond hair hanging down the rider's back, beneath a broad-brimmed black hat.

Lucy Dragoman?

She might only be looking for Cynthia. But there was a chance she'd thrown into this crazy charade with her addlepated old man. Longarm decided not to mention the girl to Cynthia. She had enough to chew on for now, and she'd need to keep her head clear for whatever happened next.

He'd like to send her back to the lodge, but she likely wasn't safe there. Not knowing what she now knows. And not with her kill-crazy uncle.

He returned to the wash. Cynthia saw him coming, and released the dapple's snout. "Who was it?"

"Couldn't tell. But they've ridden on up the canyon."

"What are we going to do, Custis?"

Longarm looked at her. She wore a worried expression on her regal, delicately sculpted face framed by wings of her disheveled black hair. She'd gotten her color back; she looked ruddy and healthy, and for that he was grateful. He wrapped his arms around, drew her to him tightly. "Don't worry. I have a couple of weapons now, and we have a horse. I'd like to go on up and fetch McCallum's mount, but since we have this one, I'm not gonna take the time. Maybe I'll be able to swing another one soon."

She lifted her chin to regard him desperately. "So, what are we going to do?"

Longarm stepped away from her to study the ridges on both sides of the wash. "We're gonna get out of here. Gonna get you someplace safe." He turned back to her and narrowed one hard brown eye. "And then I'm gonna show your uncle just how deadly human prey can be."

He saw the conflict in her eyes as she dropped them. He couldn't blame her. The man was her uncle, after all.

"Let's mount up. I think that northern ridge is our best bet. Not quite as steep, so it'll be easier for the dapple to carry us both."

When he had her in the saddle, Longarm climbed up behind her.

"What about him?" Cynthia asked, looking down at Stiles, who appeared to be just now coming around, groaning softly behind the gag. He was far enough back in the notch that only about a quarter of his long body, clad in the fur coat that Longarm had left him with to fight off the coming night's chill, was visible.

Longarm had trussed his hands and legs together so that there was no way the man could do anything except roll a few feet from the notch. He'd tied the handkerchief tightly enough around his head that the gag wasn't going anywhere, either. Not until after the man had had a chance to work on it a good, long while. Not until tomorrow, probably.

"Won't animals find him?"

"Nothing much to be done about that." Longarm gigged the dapple down the wash. "He bought his own stack of chips in this game. If he's lucky, it'll be over soon, and you and I'll be alive so I can fetch him out of there, haul him to the constable in Gothic."

"Custis, I'm so sorry," Cynthia said as he put the dapple onto a game trail that cut across the wash to the north, in the direction of the pine-covered ridge that rose toward gray, craggy peaks.

"That'll be enough of that now, girl," Longarm chided her. "You didn't know what your uncle was like."

"I know, I know. Still, it makes me feel a little better to say it." Cynthia leaned back and rested her head lightly against his chest as they rode up and out of the wash, angling north toward the deep pine forest and the stony monoliths poking their gray peaks at the faultless, late summer sky. "I'm so sorry, Custis."

# Chapter 16

They rode for one hour along the pine-forested slopes of the northern ridges, Longarm keeping a close watch on their back trail. He had no time to cover the dapple's tracks, so he knew that the hunters would be on their trail soon if one or two of them weren't on it already. Soon, they all would be after them.

They rode for another hour, Longarm pushing the gray harder than he wanted to. When he felt the horse's stride begin to weaken beneath him, he got down and walked, leading the horse behind.

They came upon several creeks threading the ravines they crossed, and there they let the horse have a short blow and water. Longarm and Cynthia drank, as well, and they nibbled Dragoman's jerky. When Longarm had filled their canteen and walked a ways to study their back trail, they started off once more.

They climbed deep into the eastern reaches of the aptly named Lunatic Mountains, up one draw and down another, Longarm now trying to follow the rockiest possible route to leave as little sign of their passing as he could. The higher they climbed, the cooler the air grew, so that late in the afternoon, seeing that she was chilled, Longarm removed Stiles's sougan from behind the cantle of the outlaw's saddle and draped it over Cynthia's shoulders.

"It's going to be a cold night," Cynthia said, shivering as she clutched the corners of the blanket around her shoulders with one hand.

Longarm continued leading the horse up a darkening draw, gray monoliths jutting high above him. "We'll stop and build a fire soon."

"A fire?" Cynthia looked worried.

Longarm glanced over his shoulder. "I think I've bought us some time. Haven't seen or heard anything back there. When we find a good spot, we'll build a fire and see what Stiles has in his saddlebags for supper."

"Bought us time for what?"

"You know for what."

"Custis, there's too many of them. You can't possibly take them all on. Let's head back to civilization. You can find help there, other lawmen."

Longarm chuffed as he continued walking. "You see any civilization out here?" He shook his head. "Gothic's too far south. No, they'll run us down sooner or later. Can't let that happen, honey. It's about time for this hunted wolf to turn and fight again, clear our back trail once and for all."

Cynthia sighed as she swayed with the dapple's stride, the horse's shod hooves ringing off rocks. "I still can't believe this is happening."

"Gotta admit," Longarm grumbled, grunting as he led the horse over a narrow spot in the rocky trail they'd been following, on which he'd spied both elk and bighorn sheep scat, "I can't quite believe it, neither."

"Custis, I'm—"

He jerked his head at her, narrowing an admonishing eye. "You apologize once more for your crazy uncle, Miss Larimer, I'm gonna make you walk!"

She gave a weary smile and lowered her eyes to her saddle horn.

"Here we go," he said another forty-five minutes later, as they climbed a steep slope through a fir forest. Ahead was a mound of gray granite resembling a giant, elongated mushroom. The arms of the mound swung out to form a semicircle, and there was an overhanging lip that would conceal a supper fire.

Somewhere near, a spring flowed, as Longarm could hear the soft rush of running water.

He helped Cynthia down from the dapple, then, as she began gathering firewood with one hand, Longarm began unsaddling the horse. As he worked, he looked over at Cynthia carrying two or three branches at a time over to the base of the stone wall. He couldn't help smiling admiringly at the girl.

She may have been the loveliest creature he'd set eyes on, with a firm, ripe, enticing figure to go with it, but she was no hothouse lily. She came from money, but she hadn't used it to hole up in a sewing room or piano parlor. She'd used it to enrich her life with adventure. All that experience had built her character and toughened her lovely hide. He knew he was going to have trouble keeping her tucked out of harm's way while he went off to confront their hunters, to give Dragoman a taste of his own medicine, and he wasn't looking forward to it.

"What are you looking at?" she said after dropping another load of wood on the pile she'd built up near the stone wall, stopping to frown at him, at once incredulous and vaguely chastising.

Longarm felt the smile stretch his lips again as he began rubbing the unsaddled gray down with the swatch he'd cut from the burlap feed bag he'd found in Stiles's saddlebags.

"I reckon I'm looking at you, Miss Larimer."

Her frown deepened as she stared at him. One eye flashed, vaguely playful. She let the stare linger on the big lawman, speculatively, as she turned and walked out into the forest for more firewood.

When he'd finished tending the horse and found a niche in the rocks in which to tie him, Longarm left Cynthia near the fledgling fire she was building, leaning low to blow on the bits of dried grass and pine needles she'd used as tinder. Quietly, he walked off along their back trail. He'd slipped Stiles's rifle from the saddle boot, and having loaded it with the shells from McCallum's pistol, quietly levered a round into the Winchester's breech.

He walked about two hundred yards back, and as the sun dropped behind the western ridges and the air cooled while night began filling this hollow that was cut into the side of a gradually sloping, forested ridge, he sat on a rock. He pricked his ears, listening carefully the way deer listen constantly, knowing they were always being stalked by something—wolves, bobcats, coyotes, even hawks and eagles.

He could pick out the slightest sounds—falling pinecones, the chuckle of water flowing out from the spring, the wind picking up along the rocky ridge crests to the south, the faint creak of tree bark as the air cooled and the pine sap hardened.

He sat there until it was nearly dark, satisfied that Dragoman was nowhere near. As he walked back toward the ridge where he'd left Cynthia and the dapple gray, he was glad that he couldn't see the fire until he was less than twenty feet from it. It snapped and popped, sending swirls of gray smoke nearly straight up, where the overhanging lip of the ridge tore and shredded it.

A good tracker could smell it within a mile or so, of course, but it was a chance he'd have to take. It was going to get cold up here, maybe down to around freezing, and he and Cynthia both needed the warmth. They also needed some coffee with which to wash down the biscuits, jerky, and cooked elk meat, possibly left over from last night's meal, that he'd found amongst Stiles's camping supplies.

Cynthia already had Stiles's dented black coffeepot on the fire, chugging away. She'd laid out Stiles's gear, including his saddle and sougan, and she'd arranged his camping gear and food pouches at one end of the fire ring.

"You've camped before," Longarm said, dropping down beside the fire and resting an arm over his upraised knee.

"Not like this." She crabbed over to him, sat down beside him, kissed his cheek, nuzzled his neck, then lifted his arm around her shoulders, holding his hand and pressing her head against his side. "How are you, Custis, poor man? I bet you're tired as hell."

"I'm doing all right."

"Do you think we'll make it?"

"Yep."

She looked up at him and smiled her admiration.

"I must say, it's an awful situation," she said, returning her gaze to the fire, "but I can't think of anyone I'd like better to go through it with."

"Same here, girl."

Longarm pulled her tight against him, and pressed his lips to her forehead. When he tried to release her, she pressed herself tighter against him and, twisting around, shrugged out of the sling he'd fashioned for her and wrapped her arms around his neck. She scooted up onto her knees and pressed her lips against his, opening her mouth and flicking her tongue against his teeth.

"Hey, now," he said.

She groaned against him desperately and shoved her heaving bosom against his chest, sliding her hands around to the sides of his head and hooking her fingers over his ears. She rammed her tongue down his throat and pulled at his hair.

His groin warmed as her bosom hardened against him, and her warm, wet tongue slithered across his own to the back of his throat.

"Can't do this," he said in a pinched voice. "Gotta keep my head—"

"Fuck me."

"No."

"Please, fuck me. I want you to fuck me so bad all of a sudden. I know it's silly as all get-out, but. . . ." She pulled back and drilled his eyes with her own, the pupils expanding and contracting with each labored breath. "Please, won't you pull it out for me? I'll suck it for you first, if you want."

"Christ, girl!"

A wicked smile spread itself across her full, rich lips, and she dropped her hands to the buckle of his cartridge belt. Ah, shit, he thought. He was powerless to stop her. His cock was already filling with blood, and his crotch was hot and tight.

She tossed aside his gun and cartridge belt, though he

grabbed the gun back and set it nearby, in case they were interrupted in this prolonged moment of dangerous irrationality. She unbuckled the belt holding up his pants and then unbuttoned the pants themselves, and a moment later his fully throbbing hard-on dropped out away from his belly.

She crouched down before him, took the aching-hard organ in both her warm, silky smooth hands, and bowed her head over it as if in prayer to the god of male virility. She gently pumped him with both hands, and then she licked the mushrooming head until he sank back, resting his weight on his arms, and gritted his teeth.

Her tongue felt like the tip of a very sharp knife taking tiny nicks out of hip. Javelins of bittersweet pain fired down his cock and into his crotch to fan out across his hips.

She glanced up at him. When her eyes met his, her expression coolly oblique and somehow infinitely alluring, she slid her mouth down, down, down until she gagged softly and her cheeks puffed out.

"All right." Longarm drew her up by her shoulders and began unbuttoning the front of her blouse. She didn't help but only knelt before him, both hands wrapped around his hammering cock, staring smokily into his eyes, her shoulders rising and falling as she breathed.

He unbuttoned the blouse down to her belly, slid it and the straps of her camisole down off her slender shoulders. Her pale, firm breasts leaped upward, bearing the faint indentations of the lace-edged undergarment. They were warm, but chicken flesh rose across them. He cupped the rich orbs in his palms, squeezed them, then lowered his head to suck each of her nipples in turn, until each was jutting desperately, as firm as just-ripe cherries.

She let her head roll back. She groaned, swallowed, sighed, and groaned again, pulling at him harder and harder until he drew his lips back from his teeth against the ache but did not want her to stop.

Finally, when he couldn't bear it any longer, he wrapped his hands around her wrists and pushed her straight back onto the blanket she'd unrolled between the stone wall and the fire. He unbuttoned her slacks and pulled them and her lacy silk underwear down slowly, slowly revealing her hips, long thighs, wonderful knees an inch at a time.

When he'd pulled both garments down past her slender calves, he slipped them and her socks off entirely. He lifted her bare legs over his shoulders, spreading them wide and holding them there with his forearms. He fingered her for a while, until he could hear the crackling wetness and she was arching her back and panting.

Then he slowly drove his hard, wanton dong between the furred portals of her cunt.

The hot wetness of her nearly drove him to madness.

He gave a shudder and, rising up on his boot toes, drove himself downward, deep and hard. He held himself there, enjoying the hot, liquid, velvety depths of her pussy as it surged against him like quicksand.

"Oh . . . oh, Custis . . ." She rose up, gently placed her hands on his face. She sucked his lower lip before slowly digging her fingers into his unshaven cheeks, raking him slowly, deliciously, and gently bucking her pelvis against him. Her cunt expanded and contracted around him. "Fuck me, Custis. Oh, fuck me good. Now . . . more than *ever!*"

He fucked her harder, better than ever.

And when they were done they both ate hungrily, curled together beside the stoked fire, Cynthia's dress still pulled down to her waist, the blanket draped over her shoulders, both of them washing down the meat and biscuits with hot black coffee.

Longarm held out a chunk of meat to her, and she tore a chunk off with her teeth, chewing like a wildcat. Chewing, she said, "I'm so famished."

"You keep eating."

Longarm kissed her left nipple, then untangled himself from her limbs and heaved himself to his feet. She groaned her disapproval and snaked her good arm around his leg, rubbing her cheek against his crotch. Her bare breasts glowed like copper in the firelight, jostling between the folds of her blanket.

"Don't go."

He tucked a lock of her hair behind her ear, pressed her head against his thigh affectionately, and ignored the stirring of the trouser snake that the warmth of her cheek, the caress of her hand evoked.

"I'm gonna scout around. We don't want to be surprised out here."

"Promise to hurry?"

"Promise." Longarm slid the revolver from behind the waistband of his trousers, held it out to her. "Can you handle this thing, if you need to?"

Cynthia looked at the gun. She wrapped her hand around the grips, glanced up at him, and curled her upper lip. "I handle yours, all right, don't I?"

Longarm winked at her, tossed another log on the fire, then grabbed the Winchester, mindful of the fact that there were only three shells in the chamber. He donned his hat, lifted the collar of his coat against the chill, and strode out away from the fire.

He circled the camp twice, stopping several times to

watch and listen. Finally, about a hundred yards out, he climbed an escarpment nestled in the tall timber and sat down at the slabs of cracked granite. He was about to light a three-for-a-nickel cheroot to smoke while he gazed out over the velvet black canyon capped in flickering starlight when he saw a soft glow to the south.

He stared at the glow. A campfire. It had to be.

He replaced the cheroot in his pocket and crabbed carefully down the escarpment, shouldering the Winchester and walking slowly, carefully south, in the direction of the fire's wan glow.

He wasn't aware of the devilish curl on his mustached upper lip.

# Chapter 17

Nearly an hour later, Longarm hunkered down behind a boulder and, clutching the Winchester in both hands, cast a furtive glance through the black, columnar pines at the ten-foot-square area in the forest which the campfire lit. Five men dressed in fur coats sat around the fire—Dragoman, Bentley, Wolf, a man whom Longarm had seen at the breakfast table but whose name he didn't know, and the man whose clock Longarm had cleaned outside the icehouse the night before, Parnell.

Parnell's bandaged ear glowed in the darkness that the firelight shunted this way and that. The fire popped and sputtered. A large, blue coffeepot sat on one of the rocks comprising the fire ring. Steam curled from the spout. Near Dragoman's high-topped, lace-up boots stood a bottle in a wicker demijohn. On the ground behind the bottle was a cognac goblet. The other men drank from tin cups. Dragoman and his son smoked stogies while Parnell had a half-smoked quirley drooping from a corner of his mouth, beneath his battered nose.

They sat in a tight semicircle on the opposite side of the fire from Longarm, playing cards. Poker. Longarm couldn't hear much of their conversation, but he could hear the jingle of tossed coins. Dragoman laughed his wicked laugh suddenly, throwing his head back. His gray beard shone above the fire's leaping flames. The insane leader of the hunting party threw his right arm out suddenly, and knocked his son's hat from his head.

As Bentley reached for his hat, he turned his head toward Longarm. The lawman pulled his own head back behind the boulder.

He looked through the trees to his left. When he'd first stolen up on the hunters' camp, he'd heard a soft snort and the grinding sounds of horses eating. The hunters' string must be picketed over there. All the men whom Longarm had seen earlier were accounted for by the fire. Still, Longarm stepped out quietly from behind the boulder and made his way slowly through the trees toward the horses.

He stopped when he saw the humped, slightly jostling shapes of the horses ahead and right. Starlight limned them, reflected in several eyes. They seemed to be picketed between two pines that stood about twenty feet apart.

Longarm took one painstakingly slow step at a time so not to evoke a frightened whinny. When he'd drawn up to within twenty feet to the right hip of the horse picketed on the picket line's far right side, he dropped to one knee. He nibbled his mustache and tightened his grip on the Winchester as he looked around, taking his time.

Suddenly, a boot crunched pine needles.

Longarm tensed and shifted his gaze around wildly.

A shadow separated from the horses and stopped just

behind them, about thirty feet from Longarm's position. There was a low sigh. Then the picket appeared to lean back from his waist, stretching and holding his rifle up high above his head in both hands. He leaned first to one side and then the other.

Longarm held still. His blood rushed in his ears.

Had he outsmarted himself here?

Lucky he'd stopped beside a broad fir. The silhouette of the tree must be concealing him, because several times he saw the picket turn his head in Longarm's direction.

Now, the man turned and strode slowly off into the timber beyond the horses.

Who the hell was this? Lucy?

Quickly, walking on the balls of his feet, Longarm moved wide of the picketed mounts, heading in the same direction in which the picket had gone. On the far side of the horses, he stopped, pressed his back to an aspen.

Dead ahead of him were the picketed mounts. They seemed unalarmed by his presence—probably because the picket had just been here, as well. Two turned their drooping heads toward him, and their ears twitched curiously, but neither sounded the alarm.

The cream barb on the far side, however, gave a loud snort.

Longarm tightened his jaws. *Shit.*

Behind him, footsteps. The picket was returning slowly, cautiously, needles crunching beneath boots.

One of the other horses snorted.

As the picket neared the mounts, Longarm stepped around the tree, breathing through his nose to make as little sound as possible. When he'd nearly circled the aspen, he stopped.

The picket stood before him, nearly concealed in the shadow of another tree. Longarm walked up on cat feet, raised his rifle like a battering ram, and jabbed the butt against the back of the person's head.

There was a grunt. The man dropped to his knees, fell forward on his face. Longarm frowned down at the elongated body. A half second before he'd brained the person, he'd caught a glimpse of long, golden hair in the starlight. He squatted down beside the body, grabbed a shoulder, and easily turned Lucy Dragoman onto her back.

The blonde's face was turned up toward Longarm's, starlight tracing the long, fine line of her nose. Her lips were parted slightly. Her chest rose and fell, but she lay limp at Longarm's feet.

The horses had turned toward the lawman and the unconscious girl. He looked beyond them toward the fire. The men were still seated around it. Only faintly could he hear their voices that were suddenly covered by another bout of Dragoman's crazy laughter.

None seemed concerned about the horses. Likely, they never would have expected that Longarm would try to turn the tables on them.

He thought through his options. He could storm the camp, but since he was outnumbered five to one, the hunters would likely take him down before he could get all of them. And then Cynthia would likely die, as well.

No, he'd have to wait and take them down later, one by one, when his odds were better. Their not having horses would up his own chances.

Besides . . .

He frowned. Besides what?

Was he, as Dragoman had suspected, actually beginning to enjoy the challenge of the hunt? The challenge of hunting men like animals? Without the respectability of a badge?

Working quickly, he dragged Lucy Dragoman into the brush. He took the shells out of her rifle, then left it on the ground near her body. He couldn't find a pistol on her. When he'd slipped her shells into his own rifle's breech, he stole back to the horses and, cooing to them gently to keep them from sounding the alarm, he cut each free of the picket line.

Wincing as their hooves began thudding as they stepped back away from him, he cut the final two free of the line, then lifted his arms wildly and shouted, *"Hyaaahhh! Get the hell out of here, ya mangy beasts!"*

His bellowing shout echoed loudly.

He triggered his rifle into the air. It sounded like a cannon shot in the quiet night.

The horses wheeled and, loosing wild, frightened whinnies, thundered off into the night, the thumping of their galloping hooves dwindling quickly.

From the direction of the fire, men yelled.

Longarm couldn't hear much of what they were yelling. He was quick to put a good stretch of distance between himself and the bivouac, heading back in the direction from which he'd stolen up on the hunters, his devilish grin growing broader with every stride.

Longarm jerked his head up from his pillow and grabbed the .44 holstered beside him. Cynthia groaned as her head slid off his shoulder. Longarm raised the revolver, rocking the hammer back.

"Hold on, hold on!"

A man's voice. Longarm blinked. In the misty dawn light, a figure hovered over him, sort of crouched, one knee bent. His arms hung down his sides; no weapons appeared to be aimed at Longarm, whose heart thudded heavily.

"Christ," he growled, voice thick with sleep. "Who the hell are you?"

"I was fixin' to ask you the same question."

Chagrined at not having heard the man sneak up on his and Cynthia's camp, Longarm pushed quickly to his feet and aimed the cocked .44 straight out from his belly. He must have gotten too relaxed, hearing Dragoman and his men stumbling around for an hour or so after he'd left their camp, looking for their horses that had likely galloped on back to the lodge. He figured he wouldn't see anything of the men hunting him for several hours and so he had time to indulge in some badly needed shut-eye.

The light was weak, the sun not yet up, but Longarm took a careful measure of the man before him. He appeared to be in his sixties, with a thick, shaggy salt-and-pepper beard and greasy hair of the same color hanging down to his neck, from beneath a red wool cap. He wore a wolf coat and patched duck trousers. His right leg was gimpy, bent oddly at the knee, and he leaned to that side on a long branch he'd sanded down, the top of which he'd padded with burlap. He didn't have a gun in either hand, and Longarm saw none strapped to his hips.

His curiosity must have shown in his eyes.

"I mean neither you or the little lady any harm," the man said in a slightly raspy voice. He looked sharply, almost eagerly, at Longarm, one eye blinking quickly, nervously. "He after you, too?"

"Dragoman?"

"Who else?"

"Yes." Cynthia had climbed to her knees. She'd fixed

her blouse against the night's chill, in spite of the fire that Longarm had kept blazing, and held a blanket around her shoulders. "You, too, I take it?"

"Yep." The stranger shook his head, stringy hair jostling about his neck and shoulders. "They hauled me out here from near Gothic a good two months ago."

Cynthia tossed a surprised look at Longarm, whose lower jaw dropped as he said, "Good Lord—are you James Thompson?"

The man stared at him, incredulity sharpening his gaze further. "How . . . do you . . . ?"

"We met your daughter and son on the train out here," Cynthia said. "They came to Gothic to look for you, Mr. Thompson."

"Oh, no." Thompson dropped his gaze and looked around edgily. He ran his left sleeve across his mouth and made his crutch creak as she shifted his weight anxiously. "I sure hope they ain't headed up this way. Dragoman— he'll do them what he did to me. No one's safe out in this neck of the mountains." He looked at Longarm again, narrowing one eye. "What'd you say your name was?"

"I didn't. But it's Custis Long. This here is Cynthia Larimer. We're in the same boat you are, Thompson." Longarm looked at the man's knee. "What happened?"

"They run me off a ridge. I fell forty feet to a ledge, though they must have figured I'd continued on into the gorge beneath me. Broke my knee all to hell. I been holin' up in a cave on the other side of the canyon, trying to mend up well enough so I can start back to town." Thompson looked around, his eye twitching in disappointment. "I take it you don't have no horses, neither."

"We have one," Cynthia said, slowly straightening and drawing the blanket more tightly around her shoulders.

"I hid him back in the niche yonder." Longarm depressed the Colt's hammer, picked up the holster and cartridge belt, and shoved the gun into the sheath. "Dragoman's out here, though he likely has even fewer horses than we do now. Last night I snuck into his camp and hazed them all off."

"You ought to have kept one. I've been waiting for a horse to wander close enough for me to catch him for nigh on two months."

"Didn't think I'd have to bother with another one. We've got the one. That'll have to be enough for now." Longarm looked the man up and down. He looked gaunt but, aside from the knee, healthy enough. "How've you been staying alive out here, Thompson?"

"Snares, mostly. Made from vines. I've eaten enough rabbits and squirrels for a while. All I've got's a bowie knife. Almost became bobcat supper, time or two." Thompson looked down at the coffeepot sitting on a rock of the fire ring and rubbed his hand up and down his grimy right pants leg.

Longarm turned to Cynthia. "Why don't you brew a pot of coffee? I think there's still some left in Stiles's possibles."

Cynthia frowned up at him. "What're you gonna do?"

"Dragoman and his men are likely still on foot—or most of them, anyway. I'm gonna take advantage of the situation."

"Oh, Custis," Cynthia said, pulling at his sleeve.

"You need some help, son?" Thompson asked. "I ain't much good, with this knee all broke up, but I'll do what I can. Anything to get back to Gothic and find my young-uns."

Longarm grabbed Stiles's saddle and saddle blanket.

"You two stay here. Cynthia has a pistol with three shots in it. If you have to use it, shoot to kill—no questions asked." Longarm winked at the girl as he headed off to the niche in which he'd stalled the dapple gray. "Unless you're shootin' at me, of course."

# Chapter 18

Parnell stopped on the rocky trail and looked up the ridge looming three thousand feet above his head. A buzz sounded, like the drone of a blackfly in mid-September. Parnell had just started to frown when the bullet smashed through his forehead and continued out the back in a great spray of blood, brains, and shattered bone.

Parnell's head jerked straight back.

Then it bobbed forward, the light in his dead eyes going out fast.

Parnell dropped the rifle he'd been holding in his gloved hands. As he began to fall backward, the echoing report of Longarm's rifle flitted around the canyon over which a gauzy mist had begun to fall just after dawn. Parnell toppled, throwing his arms out, and bounced off a boulder. He slid off the boulder and piled up at the base of it, on his side, legs casually crossed at the ankles.

The mist shone in his rat-hair coat that now served as a burial shroud.

Behind his covering boulder, Longarm ejected the spent
cartridge from the Winchester's breech and levered fresh.
Two bullets hammered the boulder as he scuttled around
to the other side. The rifle's reports, one after another,
echoed shrilly around the craggy peaks that were lost in
the low, gauzy clouds.

Longarm snaked his rifle around the side of the boulder to see the big Indian, Wolf, running a serpentine
course up the side of the ridge, heading toward Longarm.
The Indian looked up, saw Longarm aiming down his rifle,
and stopped suddenly, bringing his own Henry repeater to
his shoulder.

Longarm's Winchester leaped in his hands.

Wolf dove with amazing agility for a man his size, and
Longarm's bullet spanged off the side of the rock he'd
dove behind, spraying rock shards. Wolf's head and rifle
appeared on the boulder's opposite side. Smoke puffed
from the octagonal barrel. Longarm pulled his head back
and gritted his teeth as the bullet spanged off the side of
his own covering rock, right where his head had just been,
and thudded into the side of the ridge.

Longarm jerked his own head and rifle out from behind the boulder. He waited. If he was adhering to the
rules of the game, Wolf was out of rifle shells. Now he'd
only have a knife and a pistol, and the distance between
them—a good sixty yards—was too great for a hogleg.

Longarm had three pills in his revolver, and four more
cartridges in his rifle.

He waited, shallowing his breath to keep the rifle from
moving around in his hands.

Wolf stuck his rifle out and then pulled it back behind
the rock, trying to bait Longarm into wasting a shell.
Longarm stayed his trigger finger. Meanwhile, he could

hear another man working up the slope to his right, likely trying to get behind him. He had to take Wolf soon or they'd have him surrounded.

Stupid bastard, he thought. I should have used my shells and Lucy's shells and had a turkey shoot around Drago-man's fire last night. But hindsight was twenty-twenty.

He held his breath as he stared down his rifle barrel at the jagged, clay-colored boulder that Wolf was cowering behind. He gritted his teeth, hearing rocks rolling off to his right, where possibly two men were working their way up and around him.

The very top of Wolf's head—he wore no hat—bobbed up slightly above his covering rock as the man crabbed back to his right. Longarm dropped the Winchester front bead sight into the V at the end of the barrel, and set both two inches left of Wolf's rock.

The man's brick-red forehead appeared, then both dark eyes.

Longarm squeezed the Winchester's trigger.

*Boom!*

The man's head jerked back and for a moment Long-arm could see no part of him. Then, as he heard rocks roll-ing down the ridge above him, he saw the big Indian rolling down the ridge below the boulder he'd been cow-ering behind. Blood flew into the air around his head, painting the rocks and bits of brush. Wolf's arms and legs flapped like a rag doll's, his rifle sliding a ways behind him before hanging up in a talus slide.

Wolf disappeared over the belly of the ridge and was gone.

A gun blasted behind Longarm. The slug thundered into his boulder, just right of his hip. He whipped around. Two men—a short, bearded man in a red-and-green-striped

blanket coat and wearing a deerskin cap with earflaps, and
Bentley Dragoman—were storming down the ridge toward Longarm, both firing their rifles and gritting their
teeth.

Longarm dropped to one knee, cast aside his rifle,
and palmed the Colt he'd taken off McCallum. As Bentley and the other man ran toward him, leaping and running
around the rocks and evergreen shrubs in their path, Longarm extended the Colt, aimed carefully, and fired.

The man in the blanket coat, running ahead of Bentley and slightly to his right, bent forward to grab his left
knee as he screamed. He fired one more shot into the ground,
then hit the ground on his head, turned a somersault, and
continued rolling on down the ridge toward Longarm.

Bentley stopped suddenly, his long, curly hair bouncing on his shoulders beneath the brim of his tan Stetson
pulled down snug against his head by a chin thong. Bentley held his rifle in both hands, snarling as he aimed down
the barrel. Longarm was sliding his own Colt over to bear
down on Bentley when he heard the ping of young Dragoman's gun hammer landing on an empty chamber.

Dragoman looked at the gun, dropping his lower jaw
and snapping his eye wide in horror.

"Son of a *bitch*!" He threw the gun down like a hot
potato.

Longarm rose slowly from his knee, continuing to hold
the Colt straight out from his shoulder, narrowing one eye
as he aimed down the barrel, planting a bead on the dead
center of Bentley Dragoman's chest.

The kid held his right hand above the pistol holstered
on his right hip.

"You can try it," Longarm said. "But I doubt you'll
make it."

Dragoman stared in consternation at the lawman, the breeze lifting his damp hair and beading the crown of his hat. The bandage on his left ear was soaked and gray.

Dragoman dropped his hand to his side. "Pa!"

He turned quickly and began running down the slope at an angle, heading down canyon. Longarm had a mind to drill him through the back of a knee, but he was rather enjoying the kid's fear and humiliation. He probably hadn't known much fear out here, hunting other men on horseback and with all the odds in his favor, as well as a father to back his play.

Besides, young Dragoman would lead Longarm to Dragoman the elder. Longarm's heart hammered with unabashed excitement.

He'd damn near won.

Keeping an eye on Bentley, Longarm walked back into the nest of wagon-sized boulders and retrieved the dapple gray. He led the horse slowly, carefully down the game trail he'd followed up here earlier, when he'd led Dragoman's party into the canyon with the purpose of hunting them each down and killing them. Now, with that all but done, and Bentley run to ground, only Dragoman was left to answer for his sins.

When he gained the canyon floor, he swung up onto the dapple gray's back and racked one of his three remaining shells into the Winchester's breech. Bentley was stumbling away down the canyon floor, heading toward a bend formed by a pine-clad ridge sloping into the chasm from the left. Longarm jogged the horse up to within thirty yards and slowed him to a walk.

Bentley glanced several times over his shoulder. He wore a frightened, haggard look, and his wet bandage appeared to be turning red again. He stumbled forward.

Longarm kept one on eye on him and one eye on the surrounding ridges.

He followed Bentley around the dogleg in the canyon floor and stopped the dapple gray. Dragoman rose up from behind a boulder about fifty yards down canyon. He'd been hunkered down there, waiting. He was a tall figure in a long buffalo coat and with a feathered, gray, high-crowned hat on his head. His red face and white beard stubble stood out in the grayness.

He stood sideways to Bentley and Longarm. He'd been holding his rifle, the Bruelmann, across his chest, but now he raised it with one hand to rest the barrel across his shoulder.

"Bentley." In the dense, weathery silence, his voice sounded like a bear's brooding, menacing growl. "You were supposed to run him back toward me. Looks to me like he's done that to you."

Bentley stopped and threw his arms up in supplication. "It's over, Pa!"

Silence. Dragoman stared askance at his son.

"He done killed Wolf and Parnell. Wylie's gone, too. Shit, Pa. Can't you see?" Young Dragoman shook his head slowly as he continued walking toward his father. "It's over."

"How many shells you got left in your pistol, Bentley?" Dragoman asked in that deep, low, threatening tone.

Bentley stopped about twenty feet in front of his father. "Three."

Longarm stopped the dapple gray a good thirty feet behind Bentley. He could take Dragoman from here if he needed to. The game was over.

Longarm felt a heavy, persistent thudding in his chest. His fingertips tingled.

Very casually, Dragoman lowered his rifle and turned it

outward from his waist. Longarm extended the cocked Winchester in his hand, and his heartbeat quickened.

Dragoman's rifle spat smoke and flames. The report sounded like near thunder echoing off the ridges.

Bentley Dragoman jerked back, stumbling around as he tried to retain his footing, then bent slowly forward, clasping his arms across his belly. He loosed a great sob that sounded like a bobcat shriek.

*"Pa!"*

"Coward!" Dragoman's retort sounded like a grizzly's scornful wail.

Dragoman worked the bolt on his big hunting rifle, ejecting the spent cartridge, and plucked a fresh one from the wide shell belt wrapped around his waist, over his coat. As he slipped the cartridge into the rifle's open chamber, Longarm leaped from the dapple gray's back and dropped to a knee.

Meanwhile, Bentley was rolling around on the ground, bellowing. The large-caliber bullet had blown out his insides, had used them to paint the rocks around him.

"Hold it, Dragoman!"

Dragoman froze. He stared at Longarm. Gradually, a knowing grin shaped itself on his gray-mustached lips.

Purposefully, Dragoman bunched his lips and raised the rifle to his shoulder.

Longarm triggered the Winchester three times in quick succession. Dragoman jerked back, raising the rifle and swinging it sideways. The gun belched smoke and flames, and the canyon rocked with the report that sounded like boulders tumbling down the walls.

Dragoman's eyes jerked wide as he continued to twist around before dropping to one knee and crouching there, the rifle slowly sagging in his arms.

"Poppa!" The scream came from Longarm's left.

He turned his head in time to see Lucy Dragoman run out from behind some boulders, a rifle in her hand, her hat flopping down her back by a thong. Her wet hair hung straight down her face, with tendrils pasted to her cheeks. Her hazel eyes were bright with savagery. She had Longarm dead to rights.

He'd just started to turn when, snugging the rifle's stock against her shoulder, she lowered her head to aim down the barrel.

*Pop!*

Longarm frowned. Lucy let the rifle in her hands sag. She turned her head slowly to her left, in the direction from which the report had come. A confused expression shaping itself on her pale, delicate features, she dropped her chin slightly to look down at her side, beneath her still raised arm. Suddenly, the rifle dropped from her hands to clatter on the rocks, and she wasn't far behind it.

She drew her knees up to her chest and crossed her arms, groaning.

A figure stepped out of the sparse timber that ran along the canyon wall. Cynthia lowered the pistol that Longarm had given her and broke into a run.

"Oh, Lucy!"

She crouched over her blond cousin, grabbing one of Lucy's arms. Lucy's groans quickly dwindled, and the blond turned her head to one side on the ground and her limbs relaxed as she died. Blood shone on the side of her marten fur jacket.

Longarm walked over and put his hand on Cynthia's shoulder. Cynthia's head was lowered, and she kneaded her dead cousin's arms with both hands as though to conjure life back into her.

"What are you doing here?" Longarm scolded her gently. "I told you to stay with Thompson."

Cynthia sniffed, released Lucy's arm, and looked up at Longarm with tear-filled, pain-racked eyes. "Why, Custis? Tell me why!"

Longarm sighed and looked around at Lucy Dragoman and her father and brother. "Who knows what gets into people? It doesn't help that they were all stuck up here together, alone." He gave a soft, caustic snort. "And loved to hunt."

His own heart was finally slowing.

He couldn't deny that he'd felt some of what Dragoman had accused him of—the thrill of the hunt—but now that it was over he felt washed out and depleted. And heartsick for Cynthia.

He walked over to where Bentley and Dragoman lay still in death. He sighed again and sat down on a rock between the two men and stared across the canyon, at the dapple gray grazing the grass along the trickle run-out from a near spring, and dug a cheroot from his shirt pocket. He poked the cigar in his mouth and slipped a match out of his coat pocket.

Cynthia moved slowly toward him, holding the wool blanket around her shoulders. She looked pale, her eyes stricken.

Longarm returned the match to his shirt pocket, stood, and hugged her tightly in his arms. He held her for a long time as she cried.

Finally, returning the cigar to his pocket, he kissed the girl's rain-damp forehead, rubbed a smudge of gunpowder from her cheek with his thumb. "Let's get Thompson and start back to the lodge. We'll fetch Stiles on the way—if he's still alive."

Cynthia looked up at Longarm, sudden fear brightening her cobalt blues. "Mrs. Wannamaker . . ."

"Ah, hell, she's fine," Longarm growled. "Likely back at the lodge safe and warm and well fed." He looked around. "I'll send someone out from town to retrieve the bodies, bury 'em proper."

He was too tired to do it now. And he wanted to get Cynthia and James Thompson back to Gothic as soon as he could.

Longarm retrieved the horse and hoisted Cynthia into the saddle. He climbed up behind her. She leaned back, turned his face with her hand, and kissed his lips.

"Alma and Angus are going to be very happy to have their father back."

Longarm winked at her and booted the dapple gray slowly forward.

Sudden thunder clapped, and the rain fell harder.

"Thanks for the vacation, Billy," Longarm muttered, tipping his hat against the weather.

# LONGARM

### GIANT-SIZED ADVENTURE FROM
### AVENGING ANGEL LONGARM.

# BY TABOR EVANS

penguin.com/actionwesterns

M456AS0510